Drome Chronicles

Volume I

By Veracity Williams

Drome Chronicles

Volume I

By Veracity Williams

ISBN 978-1-387-25140-7
3rd Edition © 2017
Photos obtained by license through Adobe Stock

Printed by www.Lulu.com
Edited by Dr. Julie B. Williams

www.VeracityWilliams.com

DEDICATION

To "The Sisters" (Jacqui, San, Abby, and Deanie Brown)

Thank you for instilling in your children the importance of family and reminding us to always pay attention to and follow our Dreams!

To Robert "BeBe" Williams A.K.A Daddy,

Thank you for teaching me to be a reader! I hope you can read my book where you are. I miss you and love you forever. See you in my Dreams

TABLE OF CONTENTS

List of Characters by Family

Brown Family

Saran Moorlander: Main Character of Drome Chronicles. Daughter of Allayna Moorlander and granddaughter of Naomi "Nana" Brown Moorlander and Roderick "Papi" Moorlander

Naomi "Nana" Brown Moorlander: Matriarch of the Brown Family. Raised in New Charleston, SC but vacationed on Benaly Island as a child.

Roderick "Papi" Moorlander: Husband of Naomi Moorlander

Eryck Brown: First cousin of Saran Moorlander. He is raised with Saran by Nana since his father died while he was young. They are like brother and sister but also best friends. They are also the same age and in the same grade in school.

Kyialles Brown: She is mother of Eryck Brown

Gullivan Family

Everett Gullivan: Patriarch of the Gullivan. Dies in mysterious fire on Benaly Island many years before Papi finished the family cottage restoration.

Anya Gullivan: Everett Gullivan's sister who has a baby as a teenager and leaves Benaly in shame.

Pherron Black: The nephew of the Gullivans.

Story One:

Saran Moorlander

A TRUE DREAMER'S TALE

SARAN'S 1ST DREAM STATE

Scratch...Scratch...Scratch. Her throat was dry. Her skin itched. It was a dry day. She was trying to remember when things weren't so...dry. So...hot. She felt dusty. Everything about her was dusty now. She had dusty colored skin. Dusty colored hair. Dusty colored eyes. She lay in bed on the first day of her senior year thinking about being dry and dusty, and most importantly, how *she* was going to find water.

When the water first started to deplete, Saran didn't understand the urgency in her grandmother's actions. Her Nana was the first in town to panic. She began collecting jugs of water and storing it below the house. She began growing more plants in the basement as well - as if the jungle in her backyard wasn't enough.

Saran was younger then and all she could think about was playing outside with Eryck and Yanieyl, her best friends. She wasted water then: taking long showers, only drinking half of a water bottle and tossing the rest, running the sprinkler in the yard for fun.

Saran had been a spoiled child. Not spoiled like a brat-given everything she wanted, but spoiled in the sense that she was given the best of everything she *needed*. Her grandparents had raised her after her mother died when she was three months old. No one could explain her mom's death, but they attributed it to her having a baby at an "older" age though no one spoke of how old her mother really was when she died. One night, she simply went to sleep and never woke again. Saran had only known Nana and Papi, and she had only known the life of Benaly Island. She'd never even seen her mother's grave marker.

Their home was a small cottage near a beach on Nana's family island. Neither Nana nor Papi had been raised on the family island, but they had visited there often as children with their families. They began a courtship at an early age, but it blossomed into something "real" when they became adults.

Papi had started renovating the cottage when he was 34 years old; and it had taken him twenty years to complete it, but he did it himself with very little help from friends and family. The best part of the cottage was the story it told. The structure of the cottage was a combination of gray, black, brown, and white stones with pieces of various shades of bricks from all over the country. Papi would see stones or old bricks and collect them, bringing them back to the island whenever they visited-always adding to the original structure. Nana's family were the original inhabitants of the island and the cottage was built on the remaining structure of Nana's great-great grandmother's home which was built well before the Emancipation Proclamation of the old Americas. In other words, the cottage was a historical landmark for Saran's family. So, when Nana and Papi retired early, they moved to Benaly Island for "tha remainder of our days" as Nana always said.

Saran's room was a loft in the center of the cottage that her Papi had added especially for her. Her room covered the span of the house, and in the center of her room was her bed sitting directly in front of a balcony that overlooked the den.

In the den, there was a fireplace that sat directly in front of Nana's couch. Nana had recovered the couch so many times and Saran often joked that the couch had to be 100 years old. There were two recliners on either side of a hand-carved coffee table where Nana and Papi sat every evening after dinner: Saran watching her favorite shows on TV.

The cottage was built with an open floor-plan, so the kitchen was visible with a connecting dining area; and this was Saran's home. Her whole life had been serene and non-complicated until the water began to recede...until the beach began to disappear. She was twelve years old the summer that they began to ration the water in Benaly: the summer she had her first True Dream.

On Saran's 12th birthday, she woke feeling like she was in another place. She looked around for things that looked familiar to her. She was clearly still in the cottage, but her room looked completely different. Where her built-in book shelf used to be, there was no wall. Where there used to be a winding staircase, there was just one floor. And when Saran looked for her balcony, she realized that she wasn't on the second floor at all; she was on the 1st floor and there was no electricity anywhere. None of the modern appliances that Papi had installed were present and a small fire was built close to Saran's now make-shift bed.

Saran felt like she should be nervous, but she wasn't. She felt an overwhelming sense of home when she looked around. She tried to yell out to Nana and Papi but found she had no voice. Soon she heard a rustling near her and noticed that there was someone lying next to her in the bed. She turned and saw a girl, or maybe a young woman, with long black hair. She had honey colored skin with small, dark, almond shaped eyes. When Saran looked at her, she felt as though she was seeing her mother for the first time. She had seen pictures of her mother and this young girl looked very much like the girl in the pictures she had always cherished.

Saran called out to her, "Hello, who are you? Can you hear me? Can you see me?"

No sound came out, but the girl turned her head slowly in the direction of Saran; she did not respond. Again, Saran called out, "Are you ok? Where am I?" Again, the girl turned as if listening for Saran but not truly acknowledging her presence. The girl mouthed as though she was speaking, but Saran heard nothing. Saran got off the bed and tried to stand in front of the girl, but as Saran stood up so did the girl.

The girl began to walk around the bed in Saran's direction reaching her hands up as if to feel for Saran. Saran reached for her as well, pushing her hands in the direction of the young girl. Slowly the girls intertwined their fingers together and a resounding light blasted throughout the room. When Saran was finally able to adjust her eyesight and she realized she could feel the other girl's hands, she called out again. This time, she could hear her own voice and she knew the young girl could hear her too.

"What just happened?" the young girl replied. She had a very thick accent like she was from a Caribbean island. Saran instantly recognized the sound as the Gullah accent of the Old South Carolinians.

"I d-d-don't know. I was at my Nana's and..." Saran stopped as she realized the shock on the young girl's face.

"You sound different? Where your people from?" the young girl asked.

"I'm from here: Benaly Island. This, or at least I think this is my home. It looks different but the same too." Saran tried to explain, though she wasn't entirely sure *where* she was or how she had gotten there.

The young girl looked at Saran quizzically and explained, "I was starting to wake up when I thought I heard someone. I moved towards the sound when I felt your touch. Where am I?"

"I could actually see you lying there, but I couldn't say or hear anything. I'm not even sure where I am, but what's your name? I'm Saran...Saran Moorlander"

The girl continued to look around while saying, "I am Aline... Aline Brown."

"I have an ancestor named Aline Brown; I think she was like my great-great-*great* grandmother."

Saran started to think about what was happening to her. Maybe this was a dream? Maybe her longing for her mother had found its way into her dreams? Surely, that is what was happening. She kept pinching her arm, but she couldn't feel her own skin. She knew it was far-fetched. She knew it couldn't be true. It was just too much to process but Saran heard herself saying it aloud: "I know this is going to sound crazy, but...I think I have traveled back in time some way."

As Saran walked around, she realized that she couldn't touch anything. She reached for the mantle before her, but nothing. She tried to move to other parts of the house, but found herself stuck near the bed with Aline's hand in hers. It seemed she could only touch Aline and the shared bed they had risen from. Aline noticed Saran making these attempts and she seemed to struggle with it as well. Aline finally took a deep breath as if she was having a revelation. She turned to Saran and asked, "Saran, what does this house look like to you?" Saran began to describe the appearance of the cottage as she saw it and Aline looked on curiously.

Aline appeared baffled as she replied, "This house does not appear as you describe. I see strange lights and ceilings where there were none before. I am up high, looking down; but when I went to sleep I was grounded in my bed."

Saran smiled as she realized they had crossed rooms. Saran stood in Aline's room while Aline stood in Saran's. "I'm not sure what this means, but you are in my room,

Aline; I think I am in yours. This is so weird. I wish I could tell if I am sleep or awake." Saran pinched her arm and found there was no feeling. She then pinched Aline's arm and Aline responded with an "Owwww" and a disgruntled look.

Aline reached for the bed and was able to sit down. Aline dropped her head and began a low hum. She was clearly a young girl, but she appeared older and wiser at the same time as if she held the answers of the world in her mind. She slowly began to chant, "Qualette en motem. Balless om filay." She said this phrase over and over at the same steady pace until eventually the rooms began to merge.

Saran could not believe what she was seeing. While still looking at the room of Aline, she began to see faint shadows of the renovations on the cottage. When Aline finished speaking, she stood up and moved to a table near the make-shift bed. She motioned for Saran to follow her, and she did. They both sat at the table and Saran was shocked to see that they both appeared to be sitting and she could touch the things near her.

"Saran, I know why you sound so strange to me but I do not sound as strange to you. You are probably more familiar with the sound of our people, but I have yet to hear the sounds of yours. Do you believe in the power of dreams?"

"Uh...I don't know that I have thought anything about dreams at all. I have a lot of dreams each night and I know I remember way more dreams than the people I know, but having power? No, I didn't think dreams could do anything at all."

Saran began to think about her first feeling that she was dreaming. Maybe dreams *were* more than she realized.

"My dear, I have recorded my dreams for many moons now and have discovered that my dreams help me prepare for what is to come. The more that I make an effort to remember my dreams, the clearer they seem to be. People have come to me from far and wide to help them understand the dreams they have." Aline explained this information as though it was everyday conversation, but Saran's mind was reeling. She was beginning to get frightened and wondered if this were real. What did it look like to Nana and Papi? Had she actually left her home on Benaly or was she there? Did it look like she was she sitting in the den talking to herself? This was confusing and frustrating, and Saran had had about enough of this!

"So, you're telling me that you're a gypsy or something? Are you gonna pull out a crystal ball? And what's this gotta do with us waking up in each other's room? How are we able to sit at this table now? What are you, *exactly*??? A *witch*?!?" Saran realized that she was beginning to really panic: her chest was tightening and she felt as if she couldn't breathe. She kept trying to wake herself up; but when she tried blinking hard to wake up, when she tried to pinch herself, she was still sitting at the table with Aline.

Aline looked at Saran calmly with her young and old way, "No, my child, I used the meditation rituals of our people to bring us together. Through our blood energy, we are able to merge ourselves into other worlds. My chant was a spell of sorts, but I am no.... w-i-tch," she said the word slowly pronouncing the word delicately as if it held more meaning than she said. It was as if the word was offensive. "Witches are not held with high regard. They are thought to be charlatans. They are not in tune with their blood energy as my people are."

"Well a witch is just someone who can do magic mine."

"I understand. However, our meditations are not magic. What I have done is use my natural energy to manipulate the things around me. My people have long been in tuned with our bodies and the energy around us. Many people confuse it for magic but it is not. All living creatures possess this ability." Aline described her talents with such ease and nonchalance, but Saran found all of it to be weird and scary. As they continued to talk, the world around them began to shift.

Aline looked around nervously and began to speak again, "Saran, daughter of my daughters, you have been chosen as a True Dreamer. The fact that you are here with me proves this to be true. I am unsure how long our connection will last but I desire to tell you more of our people and what your destiny entails. Today is my 21st birthday and I am assuming that today is your 12th birthday. This day and time was foreseen hundreds of thousands of years ago: before my birth and the birth of my mother's mother. I believe that I *am* your ancestor Aline Brown"

Saran looked shocked as her great-great-great (and maybe some more greats) grandmother began to explain an ancient legend about Dreamers: people who could enter, manipulate, and predict dreams as well as the actions of the people dreaming. She talked about another world on a different dimensional plane called Drome. On the world of Drome, the Dromites learn to protect and train the Dreamers of Earth. For every Dreamer, there is a Dream Warrior. In the past, Dreamers and Dream Warriors were connected mentally, physically, and spiritually. The task of Dreamers was to keep humans evolving on Earth. Several thousand years ago, humans began to become involved in chemicals and behaviors that prevented them from remembering their dreams at night. The result was the lost heritage of Dreamers, the disconnect of Dromites to Earth, and the de-evolution of humankind.

Benaly Island was the home of the 1st Dreamer on Earth when the world was but one land mass. After millions of years, the land mass broke apart and drifted throughout the ocean. Benaly had been known by many names, and people had spent their lifetimes searching for Benaly because it was believed to have the ancestral powers that would help the Dreamers rediscover their heritage. Legend told that when the last living Dreamer returned to Benaly Island, Drome and Earth would be connected again. One human would come forth that could travel between Earth and Drome, between the past and the present, between one person's dreams and another person's. This one human would change the world as we know it and would be called: a True Dreamer.

"Saran, my father was a Dreamer and he passed on all the traditions and beliefs I have come to know. I found myself disbelieving the legend because it seemed like fairy tales Papa told to me to bring on sleep, but as I grew I knew there was truth to it. Hard to accept because it is not only a legend, but it is also a curse. But with you being here now, in front of me, looking so much like the women of my family...I know it is true. Saran, you must be careful. You are the last of the Dreamers on Earth, and you are the first True Dreamer. A True Dreamer can cross barriers and dimensions without the use of meditations or energy bending which makes you special beyond anything I am or your 'witches.' Witches in Salem and many other towns were murdered for their unique gifts and a True Dreamer is so much more than 'a witch'. A True Dreamer is the only human who can walk the planes of Drome. A True Dreamer is the only being that can save humankind from drought and famine and save Drome from annihilation."

Saran stood silently and in awe as Aline told her of a hundred-million-year-old curse on Earth and her purpose in relation to the curse. She felt fear swell inside the pit of her 12 year old stomach as she realized the importance of what Aline was describing...of the importance of who she was. Aline continued, "Many will envy you, but most will fear you. You *must* find your Dream Warrior. He will protect you and teach you the ways of Dreamers. There is nothing more important than finding him. Begin to record your dreams and begin to study dreams, but tell no one about your ability or this dream today"

"So, this is a dream?" Saran asked desperately.

Aline was still speaking as Saran felt a rush of heat against her skin and she realized that she could no longer hear Aline. As the warmth hit her, she realized that Aline was fading and so was her room. Finally, Saran looked and realized that she was alone in her modernized cottage built by her Papi, but she was not in her loft where she had gone to sleep. She was still downstairs and she was sitting on her Papi's recliner beside the coffee table. She felt her arm and realized that the warm sensation was still there. Just as she was beginning to decide that everything she had experienced was *just* a dream, she looked at her wrist. A small crescent shape was searing into her forearm. She winced as it continued to burn and develop. To the right of the crescent shape, three small dots began to appear in the shape of tiny stars. Once the heat subsided, Saran looked to notice what appeared to be a small brand of the moon and three stars fully formed and healed.

That was five years ago. That was when Saran started to track her dreams and wait for the warrior that would teach her and protect her. She never spoke about that night. She never spoke about her dreams. And she, definitely, never spoke about her growing powers.

It was now her senior year of high school. She had not met a warrior. She had no clue what being a True Dreamer meant. And she was tired of hiding and being the quiet shy girl! This year would be different. This year she would show the world who she really was!

RETURN OF THE GULLIVANS

Yanieyl Starwell ran to Saran Moorlander's door with the exciting news. Saran's grandfather opened the door as Yanieyl burst through smiling and kissing the older man on the cheek.

"Good Morning, Papi!" Yanieyl said affectionately as she raced up the stairs to Saran's loft.

"Good Morning, Yani! Where's the fire?" Papi chuckled at his own joke knowing that Yani barely heard a word he had said.

Upstairs, Saran was standing in front of her oak dresser preparing for school. "Hey, Boo!" Saran said as she saw Yani's reflection through the mirror. "Why do you look like you've been runnin' a marathon?" Saran turned around to get a full look at her best friend of 15 years.

Yani was tall by most people's account. She stood 5'8" and was entirely voluptuous. She had smooth dark skin, thick dark eyelashes, and beautiful pearl white teeth. Her hair was thick and she wore her hair down with two twists on each side to contain it. She usually wove flowers into her hair to match her outfits daily: her scent was always intoxicating because of them. Saran realized at an early age that she envied her best friend's beauty. Even in school, every boy wanted to date Yanieyl because not only was she strikingly beautiful, she was athletic and smart. When kids picked on Saran for being "weird" or for staring off into space, it was Yani that stood up for her. Saran thought of Yani like a sister; and every morning before school, Saran looked forward to seeing her best friend for breakfast at the Moorlanders. This morning, however, Yani was running a little later than usual; so Saran really tuned in when she realized how frazzled Yani looked.

"You're not going to believe the news I got!" Yani began talking between breathes as she tried to recover from her run to the house. "God! I feel like the farther away from summer we get, the more I get out of shape! Bye, bye, Summer body...Hello, Fall conditioning! So anyway..." Yani took another deep breath. "You know how I usually stop at the store to get our lattes before I come over here?" Saran nodded agreement as she continued to get dressed.

"Miss Oliver from the store was telling Sophia Johnson that there was a new family that moved to the island into the old Gullivan house." At the sound of 'Gullivan House,' Saran was on high alert. She paused for a moment but kept moving. Nana had told her many stories about the family feuds between the Browns and the Gullivans of Benaly.

Decades before Saran was born there was a major fire at the Gullivan House and it was destroyed. No one in the Gullivan family survived the fire and everyone that worked for or with the Gullivans moved away because of the pain and the memories...supposedly.

Saran felt a rush in her heart and sudden warmth on her skin. Slowly the brand on her right wrist began to burn: it was a feeling Saran had to come to recognize as her "Dreamer Sense": the feeling that a premonition would come through her dreams soon.

Normally, Saran didn't get into gossip. She didn't watch reality TV, and she avoided the town gossip as much as possible. Since her 12th birthday, things for Saran had changed and she had learned to be a private person because of her "True Dreamer" abilities. But today, just the name "Gullivan" had her curious before she even knew who was moving into the house.

"Saran?!? Are you even listening to me?" Yani had the look she gave when Saran drifted off into her own thoughts-which happened way more often than not: patience and irritation all at once.

"Ugh, I'm sorry. You know I get distracted. What'd you say?"

"I *said*, 'The Gullivans are coming back and they are bringing their nephew with them!'..." Yani knew that Saran was interested in anything concerning her family's history. Saran may not have gotten into the town gossip; but if it was about her family, she had to know. "Bet you heard that!" Yani exclaimed with a huff as she pounced on the side of Saran's bed.

The Browns were original settlers of Benaly; and for all of the information that was known about the Browns, there was an equal amount that was a mystery. And Yani had known from years of investigating with her best friend that Saran would want to know about the return of the "Gullivans."

"A nephew? I thought everyone died in the fire."

"Well, apparently, Mr. Gullivan-the one that's your Nana's age- had a sister who moved away when she was a teenager. She got pregnant and no one in their family wanted anyone to know about it. She hasn't been seen or heard from in over 60 years. The Gullivans disowned her and swore to never speak of her again. When the fire happened, they say she didn't even come for the funerals. I think that the sister's child is maybe your mom's age? Or something like that... Anyway, the point *is*, there is a nephew and he is coming to *our* school." Yani absentmindedly fumbled with her fingers and mumbled, more to herself, "I wonder if he's cute." She didn't notice Saran reaching for her wrist as she talked; she never noticed.

As Yani finished talking about how cute 'the nephew' might be, Saran put the finishing touches on her hair and they headed downstairs for breakfast. Nana was waiting downstairs with Papi. She kissed both girls and asked, "So what was with all the girlie commotion up there this morning?"

The girls exchanged looks and said simultaneously-Yani with a smile, Saran with a frown, "The Gullivans are back."

Nana's face went pale as she reached for her chair. Papi looked at his wife of close to 50 years with a slight hint of worry. They had raised Saran in their later years after their only daughter, Allayna, died. Nana was already in her 50s when she first moved to Benaly, so she'd had little contact with the feud. Therefore, she rarely thought about the Gullivans and she NEVER talked about them. And though Saran never thought about her grandparents' ages, today, when Saran looked at her Nana, she realized that it was the first time her grandmother looked "old."

"Nana, what's wrong?" Saran asked.

"It has been many years since I have thought about the Gullivans. My mother never allowed me to speak to the Gullivans or play with them when we visited the island. My grandmother despised the Gullivans. One year, I met Everett Gullivan at the grocery store..." Nana stopped as if she were weighing her words, "...he was sort of close to my age and he seemed..." she stalled again, "he was nice; but his mother saw him talking to me and she pulled him away. We grew to dislike each other as children because we were told to...it was what we knew. Before the fire, we kept our distance from each other but he was never mean to me. We had actually grown to be cordial with each other." Nana looked shyly at Papi. "There was *something* there whenever we were near each other...a strange feeling that I never could shake. No matter how old we were."

Nana didn't say another word. She simply stared into space. Papi looked on curiously.

Saran listened to her grandmother and knew instinctively that Nana was keeping something more. She decided not to push the subject and smiled at Nana while saying, "Nana, I'm sure *these* Gullivans will be cool. Nobody even knows 'em or if they know anything about the feud at all. I'm sure the past is best left in the past. Isn't that what you always tell *me*?"

Nana immediately looked up and smiled at Saran, and then Yani. "Saran, you are right. What a wise granddaughter I have!" She looked from Saran to Yanieyl. "By the way, Yani, you look beautiful in that purple dress. Now, you two, hurry off to school." Nana quickly dismissed the girls and continued on as if she hadn't been flustered just seconds before.

"Thanks, Nana. Saran, we better go. I wanna see this guy firsthand. And by firsthand, I mean the first girl he sees should be me...as I take his hand!" The girls giggled at Yani's remark. Yani could be self-absorbed sometimes but it was always lighthearted confidence. Saran looked back at her grandmother as Nana hurried into the house. Nana was up to something...keeping something. Saran would find out what!

Next to Yani, Saran's closest friend was her cousin: Eryck Brown. She and Eryck had grown up like brother and sister. While Eryck's mom worked, Nana had taken care of Saran and Eryck from birth until they both turned five years old and went to school.

Eryck was very protective of Saran... as well as Yani. He was very tall and had played football, basketball, and soccer since he was a young boy. He was extremely smart, even considered a genius by many teachers. He had sand-colored skin like Saran and thick, wooly brown hair. Eryck had thick full lips that the girls longed to kiss. His eyes were a strange shade of greenish-gray; most people thought that she and Eryck were brother and sister because they looked so much alike.

Saran, Yani, and Eryck were inseparable. They had almost all of their classes together, and they hung out after school every day. Eryck and Yani had a complicated relationship that involved break-ups and make-ups, and usually involved Saran playing mediator between her two best friends. But in the end, they simply loved each other and were like family.

At school, everyone was abuzz about the "new kid." When you go to a school with fewer than 500 students, you notice everything...especially new kids. Because Benaly Island had always been a non-commercialized tourist spot, new families rarely moved there: just retirees and local children coming back after their failed attempts living on the mainland. Thus, *no one* new had come to Benaly High School in years. There probably wasn't a soul alive that could remember the last time a new family had moved to the island, so today was going to be an interesting day.

They had only been back in school from summer break for a few weeks and teachers were already giving tests because the routine was always set. Having something rattle the routine at BHS was unheard of and quite frankly, no one was prepared for this "new kid" thing that was happening today.

When Yani and Saran walked up to the school, everyone was outside. On a normal day, everyone would already be in the building, at their lockers, in the cafeteria, in the library...milling about, but not today. Today, it seemed like every student *and* their parents were in front of the school.

In the midst of the semi-chaos was Eryck, waiting for Saran and Yani on the wall by the school's front steps. It seemed like the Browns, Moorlanders, and Starwells were the only parents who didn't "escort" their children to school on this odd day.

"Have y'all seen the new guy yet?" Yani asked when she walked up. Eryck looked at her incredulously and snuffed out a "No" before getting off the wall and walking up to Saran. The other kids nearby shook their heads no as well.

"Why exactly does she care about the new guy?" Eryck asked while pulling Saran back, tugging on her sandy brown hair.

"She wants to know if he's cute or not. And don't even get started, Eryck. You're the one that decided that *you* should be single for *your* senior year. 'See what's out there' and all," Saran mocked her cousin and then looked at him with a side-eye that told him not to push the issue.

"Well, he cain't look as good as I do!" Eryck said as he and Saran fell in step with Yani. He gave Yani a light tap on the arm, a little love-punch, and they all burst out laughing.

"Are you gonna to be a jealous ex-boyfriend this year? That would just be deliiiightful," Yani purred. Saran thought their relationship was weird, but they always seemed to be happy no matter what. Neither of them would ever admit it, but they knew that they wouldn't jeopardize their friendship with Saran no matter how often they fell in and out of love. Saran was the glue.

"What did Nana say about the Gullivans coming back?" Eryck asked the girls.

"How do you already know?" Saran asked. Eryck smiled. He never missed a beat on the island.

"She looked freaked out. She's never really talked about 'em before, you know? So, I guess I didn't expect her to say *too* much. But...the way she reacted, it was weird. And I'm pretty sure she is keeping something. Nana usually tells me everything, but she was holding back today." Saran looked at Eryck seriously. "You know I have to know what it is, right?"

Saran had her look of determination and her two friends recognized it well.

"So, *what*, exactly, do you have planned?" Yani asked.

"I was thinking about going to the old Gullivan Manor and taking a 'Welcome to the Island' basket. That would give me a chance to see inside the house *and* meet the "new" Gullivans. I refuse to accept a family feud where no one even knows how or why it started!" Saran felt her wrist warming and looked around for anything strange. "It's new people on the island! I, for one, want to meet these folks. Are y'all in or out?"

Eryck and Yani exchanged looks of worry before nodding in agreement. Of course, they were in.

Once everyone went into the school building, things began to feel normal. Saran, Yani, and Eryck headed towards the art wing. Eryck grumbled the entire way about Yani being boy crazy; Yani ignored him as usual.

"How did I let you talk me into taking art? This class is going to destroy my already messed up GPA!" Eryck liked to pretend he was dumb, but the girls knew that he had close to a 4.0 and was tied for valedictorian with Margaret Cross.

"It's supposed to be an easy A, plus you chose the last elective we signed up for: Theater Arts, which is why we all know the words to every song from that old movie, *High School Musical*. Saran likes to draw, so we are drawing this semester. And we are sewing next semester. So, suck it up!" Yani defended Saran's choice brilliantly.

While they gathered their supplies, and moved to their seats, a tall, dark, muscular guy walked into the room. He had a bald head with a full mustache and beard. "Looks like we got a sub! Boo-yah! Cake walk." Eryck leaned back in his chair and put his feet up.

Saran reached for her wrist as it began to burn unbearably. It had never hurt *this* much. The guy didn't stop at the teacher's desk; he kept walking. Her wrist began to burn more. He stopped directly beside Saran and looked down at her. She looked up at him; and when she did, she saw a galaxy of stars in the pits of his jet-black eyes: so dark, but sparkling at the same time like glitter had exploded into his pupils. All at once, a searing sensation blazed into Saran's wrist and she screamed with pain. As she grabbed her arm, the room began to spin and the last thing she remembered was the "new guy" catching her fall.

When Saran woke up, she knew that she was in a dream state. Since her 12th birthday, she'd had over twenty dreams that had taken her to her ancestors' dreams in various parts of time. Her ancestors taught her about dream states and dream interpretations, but this dream state felt different.

She was still in her school, but normally her dream worlds reversed with her and placed her in her ancestors' homes and them in hers. This time, she was actually in the nurse's office at her school. She reached for the counter to balance herself, and sure enough, she could touch it...Use it to lift herself. None of her other dream states allowed her to touch objects unless she was connected to an ancestor who knew powerful energy meditations. Saran hadn't learned those yet.

The nurse walked in and stood over her...no beside her...no both? Saran was looking at herself lying on the nurse's bed! Saran instantly thought:

> *I'm dead. This dream stuff has finally killed me and I'm drifting over my body as a ghost. Next'll be a white light and angels.*

She instantly heard a chuckle and reply:

> *No, you are not dead.*

Saran turned to see the stranger from class standing behind her looking at the other version of her lying on the bed with the nurse. She knew she hadn't spoken, but he had heard her. And he had replied, or at least in her mind he had replied.

The nurse didn't move, she didn't hear or see anything. She was busy trying to wake the sleeping Saran. Soon Saran was no longer aware of her body lying on the bed at all. Everything around her did in fact turn white and so she nervously turned to the guy beside her.

Not dead... Well, What-is-going-on?!? Who are you?!? And if I'm not dead, WHAT IS HAPPENING? This is not a True Dream, so what is it?

You are in a Dreamscape. It is believed that the True Dreamer would be able to connect to a person's dream who is not your blood relative...a person who is currently dreaming. You've connected to your ancestors in dream states, right?

Saran simply nodded.

My name is Pherron Black. I am a blood descendant of the Gullivans of Benaly and a blood descendant of the Dromite Warriors of Drome. It is my destiny to be your Dromite Warrior.

Saran jumped from the bed with a scream and the nurse dropped everything she had in her hands. Nana and Papi were standing behind the nurse in complete shock.

"We just called the... Don't move.... I..." The nurse was stuttered while looking at Saran: one hand firmly on Saran's ankle and the other moving quickly over the table grabbing papers. The nurse looked as if she had been crying; Nana *was* crying; and Papi looked like he had seen a ghost. Saran replied, "I don't need anything. I'm fine. I'm ok now. I just got weak for a minute."

Eryck, who was by the window standing unseen, was the one to speak, "Saran, you flat lined. The nurse pronounced you dead an hour ago. We were coming back to get your body."

Saran was shocked. Her family all stood in amazement and fear... Crying tears of joy and terror... Looking at Saran like someone they missed but were afraid to touch at the same time. Saran reached for her wrist and realized that it had changed. What was just a brand of a crescent moon and three stars had turned to a crescent moon with a thin outline around it and the addition of a fourth star. Saran held her wrist as her loved ones crowded her, hugged and kissed her, and began to question the hour she died.

BACK FROM THE DEAD

"How do you feel?" Nana asked Saran for the thousandth time. It had been a few weeks since Saran had "died." Everyone on the island was talking about it. The day that Pherron Black came to Benaly High was eventful to say the least. Saran hated the attention her Dreamscape had caused; it prevented her from reaching out to Pherron, the great-nephew of Everett Gullivan and her long-awaited Dream Warrior. For five years, Saran had waited to meet him, for him to teach her and train her; and now, she couldn't even talk to him.

No one knew what had happened to her and she couldn't share it with anyone, not even her two best friends. She felt horrible being stuck in the house with Nana and Papi watching her every move...waiting on her to fall out at any moment. She knew that Nana wanted to ask her more, but Saran avoided her and gave her vague answers when she asked about that day. So much about her dreams, the dream-states, and now the Dreamscapes were a mystery to her. She had learned about her dream states from her ancestors, but they had never affected her outside of her dreams. Occasionally, she would sleep walk and end up downstairs instead of in her loft, but she never felt sick or weird: they felt like normal dreams. And since she had been keeping everything "dream-related" a secret, there wasn't anyone she could ask about what she did while she was in a dream state.

But, the Dreamscape was different. They brought a person in the here-and-now into the dream with her and apparently made her appear dead to those around her. What was worse was the fact that she didn't seem to be able to control either the dream-states or the Dreamscapes.

There were several things Saran was starting to realize that made her more nervous than she had been before when she had been waiting for her Warrior:

1. She wasn't just connecting to her ancestors in her dreams anymore, they were evolving into something bigger than even her family had experienced.
2. The Dreamscape had caused the brand on her wrist to change and grow like her first True Dream, so something major was about to happen in her life. Maybe even a new power?
3. And, Pherron knew her...he was able to enter her mind. He was her Warrior. And she was more anxious than she had expected.

She knew she had to talk to him. She had to understand more. She had to get out of the house!

"Nana, I promise, I'm ok. Can I please go back to school? I was probably dehydrated. Our water rations have gotten smaller and smaller over the years. Even the ocean is getting smaller and the island bigger." Saran tried to distract her grandparents from the fact that she had been declared dead. She continued to plead for what seemed like an eternity to go back to school or at least go to her friends' houses.

"Saran, we still don't know what happened to you. You *flat-lined*. We watched it. It wasn't dehydration. We have seen that before in others. What if this *thing* happens again? What if it is something like what happened to Alla..." Nana broke off. Saran knew that Nana was thinking of her mother, but she continued anyway. She had to get out of the house.

"What if it happens while I am here? Will it make any difference? We don't know what happened, but we do know that I'm still alive and I should be living my life!" Saran realized that she was raising her voice, something she never did when she spoke to her grandparents. And she definitely didn't want to hurt their feelings in a time like this.

"Naomi," Papi interrupted them with his calm and gentle voice, "I think it is time to let her go out. She misses her friends and getting back into a normal routine may be good for her. We aren't going to find out anything new by holding her hostage in this house."

Nana shot Papi the look of death when he said this, but finally she let out a deep sigh and said, "So be it." She turned around with a huff and walked to her room. Papi moved to Saran and placed his hand on her shoulder. Saran couldn't shake the feeling that Nana knew more than she was saying.

"She means well, Saran. We never knew why Allayna died so young. The doctors could never explain it. When we thought you were gone, it brought back so many memories and so much pain. So many unanswered questions. I thought she would never breathe again: To lose you would kill her. And when you woke up...when you came back..." Papi got choked up, but continued with "she means well, my daughter, she really means well." Saran looked at her grandfather, the only father she had known, and smiled. She hugged Papi very tightly and whispered in his ear, "I'm still here, Papi, I'm still here." With that, he released Saran and she walked towards the door of the house.

She had been trying to get out of the house for days and now that she had the chance, she was actually nervous. She stopped at the doorknob. Should she go straight to school or to

Yani's house? Should she call Yani, or Eryck, first? She decided
to do neither. She still had 30 minutes before school started so
she decided to go where she had been itching to go since the
news broke: the Gullivan Manor. It was a five-minute walk
from her house and even less to get from the manor to the
school. She had plenty of time to at least talk to Pherron, and
they could walk to school while they discussed what happened.
Like Nana, she still had questions of her own.

     Saran had never been on Gullivan land. After the
mysterious fire, most people stayed away thinking it was cursed
or at the very least, haunted. She knew that her family had been
enemies of the Gullivans; and though she always wondered
why, she never dared go onto the land itself... especially after
learning firsthand about dream powers and ancient curses.
When they returned a few weeks ago, a burning desire to snoop
around and investigate the family took over her mind. She
knew that there was a story to be told, but she never suspected
the Dream Warrior that she had been waiting for would be a
Gullivan.
     After her experience at the school, she was scared of
what this relationship would bring out. Did the feud between
the Browns and the Gullivans have something to do with their
heritage as Dreamers? Would a new feud begin with Saran and
Pherron's connection? Did the Gullivans pose a danger like her
ancestors had warned her of so many times before in her dream
states?
     As Saran walked up the steps of the large mansion, she
thought of all the mysteries of her family... the mysteries of
Benaly in general. While engulfed in thought, the door to the
manor opened and a large woman with red hair came storming
down the steps.
     "I will not work in a house where I am not respected!
You people are crazy!" The woman stormed past Saran without

an "Excuse me" or a glance in her direction. She seemed to be writhing with anger. Her face was as red as her hair, her hands were clinched, and she was sweating profusely. Behind her was the tall young man from school: Pherron Black. He looked straight passed the angry woman directly to Saran.

Immediately she felt the euphoric sensation she'd felt the day he came to Benaly High. Praying she wasn't about to pass out again, she looked up at Pherron.

"Hello, Saran. Welcome back to the land of the living!"

He seemed to smirk as he said this, and at that moment Saran realized that the initial sensation she felt had quickly turned to anger. In the back of her mind, she wondered what happened with the woman who had just left. And, why was he smiling? She thought that she would feel something spectacular when she met her Dream Warrior; instead, she felt a sense of aggravation when he spoke to her. She couldn't explain what bothered her so much about him.

"I really don't see anything funny about me dying. People were freaked out by that Dreamscape. Did you *cause* it?"

"First, you were not and are not dead." He rolled his eyes as he continued, "Second, I can no more cause a Dreamscape that you can prevent them right now. So, now that that's clear, how may I help *you* this morning?" Pherron looked so nonchalant, like nothing strange had happened between them. As a matter of fact, he looked like she was inconveniencing him and it really pissed Saran off.

"I want to know more! I want to understand what is going on. I want to have answers for the people I love." Saran was visibly agitated at this point. "You show up and I pass out, have a dream where I'm watching my own body sleep with you standing by my side, and *then* I find out I'd been pronounced dead for over an hour! That's a lot to take in, even if I am a *True Dreamer*! And I would *think* you were here to help NOT agitate me!"

Looking bored with the conversation, Pherron said, "What do you want to know, Saran?" and he began walking back towards the entrance of the manor. He said her name like he had known her for years and even *that* agitated her.

"Where are you going?!?" Saran demanded angrily.

"Inside my house to get dressed for 'school'." He emphasized the word 'school' like it was a joke.

"I'm not coming in there!" Saran replied exasperatedly.

"Suit yourself, I didn't actually ask you to come in by the way. Apparently, I have to attend school here. It's the *law*. And at the moment," Pherron made a downward motion, "I don't think I'm dressed appropriately for *your* school."

At this, Saran took a moment to actually look at Pherron. He was standing in a white tank top that showed his muscular arms and tribal tattoos; and he wore flimsy, black pajama pants. Not that she normally noticed things of this nature, but he didn't seem to have on underwear. With that image, she blushed and suddenly became very self-conscious and embarrassed.

"Oh...uh...I mean. Sorry, I didn't notice that you...Ooookaaayyy, well, I will just see you at school and we can talk later?" She stumbled over her words as she backed away from the house. Pherron laughed a low, cocky chuckle and walked back up the steps going in the house without another word. When the door closed, Saran was left standing in the yard with her mouth open. She gathered herself together and turned to leave. As she turned, she saw a gray Lincoln pull into the driveway and her grandmother sat staring at her questioningly.

"What on God's green Earth are doing at this house?!?" Nana spoke through her teeth, the way she did when Saran was a little girl misbehaving in church.

"Um...I..." Saran couldn't think of a lie fast enough.

"Do-Not-Lie-To-Me Saran Moorlander! Why are you here?" Nana had never looked at Saran like this before. This was more than a you-aren't-doing-the-right-thing look. This was a you-royally-screwed-up look, one reserved for the bad kids in church...not her.

"Well, Pherron was the one who picked me up and took me to the nurse that day. And uh...I wanted to see what he noticed. I mean, I *am* just as curious about what happened as you are." Saran said as much as she could and still be truthful. She did want to know what happened; she just couldn't tell her grandma that he had come to her during that hour of her death. She couldn't say that what was an hour of horror for them had only been 5 to 10 minutes in her mind.

"Saran! You have never been a liar, so don't start now. You have no business at this house and you know it!"

"Why are *you* here, Nana? You never talked about the Gullivans before and you've been acting strange since the morning you heard they were back. I'm telling the truth...YOU aren't!" Saran walked away towards the school which was only a few blocks away. She'd never been disrespectful to her grandma and she didn't dare look back to see if Nana was following her. She didn't hear the car start, so she knew Nana was going in the house. Saran wanted to know why, but she wouldn't find out right now. She'd have to wait. She knew she had crossed a line with her grandmother. Unfortunately, she would have to explain eventually, but she wasn't sure how she could.

Walking into the school was much harder than she expected. Before she could even get to the school grounds, the walkers were whispering and looking at her suspiciously: "The girl who came back from the dead."

Saran held her head high and continued up the steps. People had always thought Saran was strange or weird, and so she rarely worried what people thought of her. However, today she felt like she should have called Yani or Eryck first. She should have called them both; she needed her friends. She was on display with no support. They had been there for every major event in her life, except the dream states. They knew every secret in her life, except the dream states. And now, they wouldn't know anything about what happened to her, especially the Dreamscape. She hated keeping secrets, especially about her dreams.

She walked to first period and sat at her desk. Yani and Eryck were not there yet and she couldn't help but wonder where they were. Eryck always came to school early, and surely Yani would come early as well since she hadn't been coming by the house for breakfast.

Soon, the room was filled with her classmates *except* for her two best friends. Once the bell rang and they still were not there, Saran began to regret coming to school at all.

"Good morning, Class!" Mr. Ostosky began the art class that Saran had made Yani and Eryck take. As soon as Mr. O began to speak, she realized that Pherron was not there either. Deep down, Saran knew that it wasn't a coincidence that all three of them were absent, but she didn't linger on the thought. "Let's take a moment to welcome back Miss Moorlander." He looked in her direction and nodded, "We're glad you're feeling better." Everyone looked and became as uncomfortable as Saran.

After about 15 minutes of everyone staring at her and paying no attention to the clueless Mr. O, the door opened and to Saran's surprise Yani, Eryck, and Pherron all entered the room-not one of them making eye contact with Saran. Yani looked like she had been crying, Eryck looked angry as if he'd been fighting, and Pherron...well, Pherron had a smile on his face and looked like a confident warrior coming from battle. When Yani sat down next to Saran, she looked with shock as she realized that her best friend was in the chair beside her.

When she saw Saran, she couldn't fight her emotions and she gave Saran a fierce hug and whispered in her ear, "I'm so glad you're back!" Saran finally felt at ease as her best friend hugged her and wept quietly.

As Saran pulled away from Yani, she began to feel a tingling on her wrist. She looked at Pherron and he smiled at her. He was moving his finger in circles around his wrist in the same area where Saran's brand had developed five years ago. She continued to feel the tingling sensation, but unlike other times, her wrist did not burn or heat up. This was a cool sensation and tickled slightly; in fact, it was quite pleasant. She shot Pherron a look and he stopped. Immediately, the tingling stopped.

What was that?!? Saran thought to herself.

It was me giving you a smooth tingle. Something to calm you.

Saran jumped in her seat as she heard Pherron's smooth deep voice in her head. His lip turned up in a cocky smile while Yani looked at her with fear, and mouthed, "Are you ok?" Saran could see that everyone in the room had noticed and they were all getting nervous, including Mr. O.

"Saran, are you ok?" Mr. O asked.

"Yes, sir. I just had a chill. I'm *fine*." She stressed the word "fine" to reassure *everyone* in the class that she wasn't about to die...again. At least, she didn't think she was.

"Ok, well on to the new project that we will be working on for the next few weeks. We are going to start working with oil paints..." Saran stopped listening and began to think again about the guy talking in her mind.

So, can you hear me right now? Saran thought.

Yes. He replied.

Can you always hear my thoughts? Little violating, don't you think?

Pherron spoke to her mind and his words were soothing to her.

I can only hear you when you want to be heard. As easily as you let me in, you can also push me out.

Push you out? But how? I feel like you have some kind of control over me. Over my thoughts and my...even my emotions.

Saran felt uneasy at the thought of him in her head. Could he see her thoughts too? The ones that lay below the surface of her mind. Could he sense the feelings that she felt when he wasn't around her?

As you become more in tuned with your Dreamer powers, you will be able to call for me when you need me and block me out when you don't. Right now, you need me whether you realize it or not which is why I can hear you now. Your friends will realize this soon as well.

He looked at Eryck and chuckled low as he had at the mansion.

Eryck became visibly angry when Pherron chuckled, and Saran began to wonder what had happened this morning to cause them to be late. The end-of-class bell rang, and all of the students got up to leave except Eryck, Yani, Saran, and Pherron.

"Saran, may I walk you to your next class?" Pherron asked formally like he was from the past. Something about him was intriguing and infuriating at the same time. The way he spoke and carried himself presented more mysteries and more questions than she was receiving answers, but she ultimately felt an undeniable draw to him.

"She *has* friends, man. She don't need you walking her anywhere. As a matter of fact, stay away from her. I don't know what you did to her that day, but stay-away-from-my family!" Eryck growled.

"Eryck!" Saran was shocked. Just as she was about to tell Eryck that Pherron had done nothing to her, Yani grabbed

Saran by the arm and pulled her down the hall with Eryck following close behind.

"What-was-that-about?!?" Saran practically yelled at her friends.

"He is bad news! The guy comes in and looks at you and then you just fall out. He picked you up and took you away and no one knew where you were. Don't you know *anything* about that day?!? That guy did something to you. He killed you!" Eryck was screaming at the top of his lungs.

"Eryck, I'm right here. Clearly, he didn't kill me. He took me to the nurse," she looked from Eryck to Yani. Neither of them spoke. They both looked down. Saran quietly asked, "Didn't he?"

Yani looked like hell run over. "No, Saran, he didn't. He took you outside somewhere. We found you at the base of the Massive Tree near the beach, and he was nowhere to be found. No one has seen him since that day. Not in school. Not in town." Yani looked at Eryck, who had begun to pace rapidly back and forth. "This morning when we got to school, he was walking in like nothing happened. Eryck hit him and that's why we were all late."

"You hit him! Eryck, why?" Saran felt like her world was spinning.

"Why?!? Why? She wants to know why I hit the man that killed...or tried to kill my... my cousin...MY SISTER! You are incredible right now."

"Eryck, Nana and Papi haven't told me anything about that day. All I know is I was in class and then you guys were talking about I died. I didn't think Pherron had anything to do with it. I thought he saved me!" Saran looked at her cousin, pleadingly...hoping he would understand and see that Pherron was not a threat. At least, not that she could see. He was her Warrior. He was sent to protect and teach her. She had been waiting for him since she was 12 years old. He was the only person she could trust with her secrets and she needed her family and friends to trust him too.

"Pherron! You say his name like he is a friend. You say it like you know him. You don't know what he did to you!" Eryck was furious and there was no sense in talking to him now.

"There's a reason our family doesn't fool with his family! There's a reason they hate each other. We're good people and they're bad! Clearly, our ancestors knew more than us! Why would you think anything else?!?"

At that moment, Nana and Papi showed up in the hall. Nana looked furious and Papi looked worried as they both looked at the children they had helped raise for many years.

"Guys, you're causing a scene. We got a call that something happened this morning. Yani, go on to class; I've already talked to your folks. Eryck and Saran, you're coming home with us." Nana spoke in her "formal business" tone: the voice she used with business men to show them she was smart and could do anything they did. It was a voice Saran hated. It was nothing like the warm woman she had grown to love and care for as a mother. Saran knew that things were only going to get worse by the tone of her Nana's voice.

"Eryck, what were you thinking?!? We have gone decades without a fight with anyone in that family, even before the fire! We could have started fresh with the Gullivans. We didn't need another feud. Do you know how many of our family have died fighting these people? Do you?!?" Nana was in rare form. She was yelling at everybody.

"And, you!" She rounded on Papi. "Let her go to school...Let her out the house...It will be good for her! First thing she does is go to that boy's house!" Papi and Eryck turned to look at Saran with shock and horror.

"You...you went to his...you went to his house?" Eryck looked pale as he reached for a chair and sat down. "You don't know this guy. You don't know anything about him, and you go to his house? Without me? Without Yani? Alone? Do you understand that you died?!? That for an entire hour we had to think about life without you? And it was all his fault!?!" Eryck began to cry unapologetically. He wept in his hands and shook his head as he tried to understand.

Saran didn't know what to do. She didn't know what to say. She looked at her family; and as she thought about what to say to ease their pain, she felt her brand begin a tingle the cool sensation that felt so pleasant before. She looked around for Pherron but knew he wasn't there. In her mind, she heard his familiar voice: *I was destined to guide you, teach you, and...love you. You are my responsibility and I was born for you. It will be hard, but we will do this. We will do it together. Stay strong for I am never far. I am Pherron Black of the ancient Dromites! I am a prince among my people, but I am forever your Warrior!*

With his reaffirming words, Saran said words that her family could never prepare for...words that would change everyone and everything in her life...forever. She looked at Nana, at Papi, and finally at the boy that had always been like her brother. She looked at Eyrck and replied, "I...I love him!"

She said it, and she knew it was right and it was real.

THE NEED TO TRAIN

"I...I love him!"

She said it, and she knew it was right and it was real. Saran looked at her family sitting before her, dumbfounded at this strange revelation. Saran realized what she said and instantly covered her mouth from self-shock. What had she said? What had she done?

"I can't do this." Eryck stood up and walked out of the house without another word. Nana dropped to her knees and Papi continued to stare at Saran with his hand on his wife's shoulder as she began to sob.

"I know it sounds crazy. I know I really don't know him. I know everything that has happened since he came here has been just," Saran searched for the word, "...unexplainable. But I also know with every fiber of my being that I truly love him. We have a connection that I can't explain and if I did, you...you wouldn't understand."

Nana stopped crying immediately and looked up suddenly. Her voice changed. It was strong and hard. It was wise and knowing. "You think I'm stupid, Saran Moorlander!

You think I don't know what has been going on in your life for the past five years. You think I don't know you have been dabbling in dream mystics! I know! I have always known. I knew before you were born! I knew when your mother breathed her last breath exactly who and what you could be! You, little girl, are the one who doesn't understand a thing!" Naomi Moorlander looked at Saran as if she wasn't her only granddaughter. She looked at her like she was a stranger, and Saran instantly felt a searing pain on her wrist.

"You knew?!?" Saran felt a stir of emotion. "You knew what was happening to me and you didn't say a word! You knew everything?"

Nana reached for Papi and started to stand up, but a force pushed her back down.

"No!" Saran heard her voice, but she felt the power of it more than anything. Her anger began to well inside of her. "You-knew-all-this-time! You let me go through this alone! I have gone through *so* much!"

"AHHHHHH!" Nana screamed as pain coursed through her body. Papi looked at Saran with fear, not understanding what was happening to his wife.

"Sa-ran, please...stop...you are..." Nana could barely say a word. As she struggled to stand, struggled to breathe, struggled to look...Saran's hand began to glow just below the brand on her wrist.

"Don't...you see...what...what you are...doing," Nana breathed out. Papi reached for Saran as she held her hand out towards her grandmother.

"Saran!" he pleaded. "Stop! You're hurting her."

Saran blinked several times to see the glow fade from her hands and her grandmother collapse on the floor. When she finally regained her composure, she realized that Nana was no longer moving. In fact, she wasn't breathing at all.

"Oh my God! What have I done?!?" Saran ran to her grandmother, but Papi stopped her, looking at her as if she were a demon.

"Do-not-touch-her! I don't know what is going on or...what you are, but stay away from her." Saran realized that everything was changing in that moment. Her grandfather didn't recognize her anymore as the little girl he had raised. She was something more. She was something bad. Saran turned and ran out of the house.

She ran and ran with no destination in mind until finally she stood at the bottom of the steps of Gullivan Manor. Pherron Black stood at the top of the steps waiting for her, as she knew he would. She ran into his arms and cried: losing herself in his arms...worrying about what she had done to the only people she had known as parents. Would they ever forgive her? Could she ever forgive herself? *What* had she done? *Who* was this boy that had changed her life in such a way in such a short time? Saran didn't know who he was or who *she* was, and she was truly terrified.

When Eryck arrived at Gullivan Manor, he didn't know what to expect. He wanted to confront Pherron. He wanted to know what he had done to Saran to make her pass out, make her flat-line, make her turn against her own family. When he walked to the house, he wasn't prepared to see Saran standing on the steps in Pherron's arms.

"Really?!? Saran, get-down-here-NOW! Get away from him!" Eryck yelled possessively as he began running towards the house. "What are you doing *here*?!?"

"Eryck, I know you don't understand, but I have done something so terrible. Nana..." Eryck cut her off before she could finish.

"Saran, I thought about what you said and I know that he has given you some kind of drug. I know it isn't *you* who thinks all this crazy stuff. And we're going to get you some help. I promise. But you have to get away from this guy!" He was begging her; he was pleading desperately. Eryck's eyes were puffy from so much crying and his nose was red; his face was red. He was frustrated and angry; Saran could see his pain, but she could also *feel* it.

Saran looked at Pherron and knew that she had to get control of the situation. "I need to go with him. I need to make it right with my family.

"I understand. I am here. I am here for you, always. Go to them." Pherron looked at her with star-filled eyes and placed a light kiss on her forehead.

Eryck gasped as Pherron kissed and hugged his cousin. It took everything in him not to charge the stairs, punch Pherron, and take his cousin away. But he stood and watched silently with his hands clinched and his mouth closed tight. He didn't want to do anything that would make her change her mind about leaving. He had a plan and Yani was on standby to put it into effect. He had to get her away from that house.

Saran ran to Eryck, hugged him, and left Pherron behind. Eryck smiled at the warmth of his cousin...his sister...his friend. He would save her from Pherron Black. He would always keep her safe.

Saran and Eryck walked in complete silence. Saran knew where they were going. They were heading to the Massive Tree on the beach, or what was left of the beach. Since the water had begun to recede five years ago, the Massive Tree had become a place for Saran, Yani, and Eryck to escape. It was the first place that Yani and Eryck looked when Saran had passed out and apparently where Pherron had taken her.

She had been lying at the base of the tree that day, barely breathing when they found her. It wasn't until they moved Saran from the tree that she'd stopped breathing all together. They were so scared that they raced her to the school nurse because it was so much closer than the mainland hospital.

Eryck had carried guilt with him since that day because he felt that her 'supposed death' had been his fault. He felt as if he had failed her as a cousin and a brother. Now, he was more protective than ever.

As Saran and Eryck approached the tree, Yani was there waiting for them with a picnic basket and blankets. Saran knew that all of this had been planned before she accidently attacked her grandma, so she didn't say anything immediately. But she knew...she knew she would have to tell them both what she had done. She was tired of the secrets. She didn't want to feel ashamed of her powers, and keeping them a secret had led to her harming the one woman she loved more than anything; so shame was exactly what she felt.

"She was with Black at the manor," Eryck said to Yani as they approached. Yani looked horrified.

"First, why were *you* at the manor? You were supposed to be going to Saran's house." Yani didn't take her eyes off of Saran.

"I wanted to talk to this dude. Tell him once and for all to stay away from Saran. He's done something to her. I couldn't tell you on the phone, but she said she loves him!" Eryck looked at Saran for confirmation. Yani looked at her, too, in anticipation of denial.

Saran simply looked down.

"Tell me he's lying. Tell me he's confused. How could you love him? You don't even know him? You've seen him like twice and one of those times he hurt you!?!" Yani wasn't yelling, but Saran could hear the crisp sharpness in her voice indicating her anger.

"Ok, so...There are just so many things that I need to tell you. So many things that I have kept from you for so long...kept from both of you." Saran started, but she just couldn't figure out how to explain this to her friends. She wanted to show them her power, but she couldn't. She couldn't control her powers nor did she know what she could do with them. After hurting Nana, she was scared to try anything.

Now is not the time. Saran heard in her head. She wanted to shake the sound out of her ears. She wanted to ignore her warrior, but she knew that she couldn't.

"We're your friends, Saran. We're your family. What have you kept from us? I thought you told us everything?" Yani looked betrayed and hurt. She looked confused and scared. "You know what, Saran, it doesn't even matter. We love you no matter what. You can tell us anything and that wouldn't change."

Saran looked at her friends...her family and knew it was true. She knew they would support her. But would they believe her? They already thought that Pherron was causing everything. How could she tell them that it wasn't Pherron at all? "I don't know how to explain everything to you." Saran felt her wrist tingle. The feeling was a dull throb she had never felt.

Now-is-not-the-time! Pherron seemed to be forcibly entering her mind. He'd said that she could push him out and she wanted so desperately to do that now. She tried to focus on talking to her friends. She tried to ignore the urgency of his tone in her head, and it seemed to work.

"I did something today. I did something to Nana." Saran began, and as she started to talk, she felt woozy. Everything began to spin around. Her wrist throbbed incessantly... to the point that the pain became unbearable as Saran watched her friends fade into darkness.

"Saran! What's happening?" Eryck was reaching for her, but she couldn't respond. Yani jumped up with her cell phone and began calling someone.

"We have an emergency on the beach. We need a truck here, now!"

Those were the last words that Saran heard before she was consumed with darkness.

I told you that now was not the time!

Saran looked to her side and saw Pherron standing near her looking agitated.

Everything around them was water. The Massive Tree was still there but majority of the land had disappeared, consumed by the water surrounding them. They were standing on a tiny island with the Massive Tree and nothing else. Saran could see her body lying on the ground at the base of the tree. Pherron had one hand on the tree and the other holding Saran's hand at the same time. She could feel his touch and his touch calmed her, though he was visibly upset.

What's happening now? Are we in a Dreamscape? I want to tell my friends and family what is going on!

As Saran talked to Pherron, she felt a tugging pain near her heart. *Owwww!* She screamed, or she thought she screamed, but barely a whisper escaped her. She did, however, feel *real* pain in her chest.

They are trying to move your body. I am keeping it here. When they try to move it, I have to slow your heart. They are trying to revive you and that is the pain you feel. While you are attached to me in this Dreamscape, you cannot live in their world. You are straddled between Earth and Drome. Something no human should be able to do, but you...you are the True Dreamer. Because you have not learned to use your powers, you cannot be in both places as I can. They think you are dying again.

I want to go back. I have to go back! I want to talk to them. They deserve the truth. Everyone deserves the truth. Nothing good has come from me lying to my family. And these powers HURT Nana today. I actually hurt her. I don't know what has happened to her or if she even survived it! Send me back, NOW!

Your Nana is alive and well, but you knew that in your spirit or you wouldn't have come to the tree. Naomi is a strong Dreamer, though she has tried to deny her heritage. You need to train. You need to learn how to be in both worlds. You need to become the True Dreamer you are destined to be.

But how can I do that? I can't do this without them. They are my world.

I am your world! And, it is not safe to tell them about your powers. They will not understand. They will not accept you!

You don't know them! You don't know the love they have for me. I know I can make them understand. I can show them. I can enter their dreams and show them.

You can barely enter my dreams without my help. Do you see how they treat me? They don't even trust you or your feelings!

And you think they should? I know that we're destined to be together...or whatever. I can feel the truth in that. I've waited for you for five years. But... they don't know that. They don't know anything!

Saran looked down in frustration and became absorbed with the water surrounding the Massive Tree. She hadn't seen so much water since she was a small child. She was instantly mesmerized and wanted to touch it. She forgot about the debate with Pherron and soon she was reaching for the water;

she released Pherron's hand. He tried to stop her but couldn't. He screamed in agony: *Nooooooo!*

Immediately, Saran was at the base of the Massive Tree with people surrounding her, not the beautiful water she was longing to touch. Yani and Eryck were holding each other crying hysterically. Nana and Papi were there standing behind several emergency people. Saran sat up with a jerk and everyone around her gasped. She wondered if she had flat-lined again like before.

Nana held her breath and moved towards her. She reached apprehensively for Saran. Saran could tell her grandmother was scared of her, but her unconditional love was still undeniable. She could see concern and fear in her eyes. Concern for the safety of her granddaughter and fear of what her granddaughter could do. Nana leaned down to Saran and whispered in her ear, "Do-not-say-a-word." Saran looked at her grandmother and nodded in agreement.

"Ma'am, your granddaughter is breathing fine now. All of her vitals are reading perfectly. It's as if nothing happened. We'd like to take her to the hospital and admit her. This is the strangest thing I've seen in my forty years of healthcare!"

Yep, died again.

Papi stepped up immediately and said, "I don't think she'll need to be admitted. We really want to get her home." He seemed better than the last time Saran had seen him. He wasn't looking at her like she was a demon from hell; he looked at her like her Papi who loved her more than anything.

The paramedic looked at all of Saran's loved ones carefully and shrugged, "Are you sure? This is *very* strange and you may want to have her monitored for..."

"No, we're ok. Saran, how do *you* feel?" Nana peered at Saran with tight eyes and spoke with the "business" voice.

"I'm fine, Nana. I can get up now. I think I was just dehydrated." Dehydration was always a good excuse with the water depletion. Saran looked at Yani and Eryck to see if they were buying it, but they barely made eye contact with her.

"Ok, if you guys will sign this ambulatory paperwork and a liability form for her to be released from our care without transport, we'll get out of your way." The paramedic gave another cursory glance at Saran and went for the paperwork. Papi reached for Saran to help her stand up. Yani gathered up all of the things they had brought to the tree. Eryck began to walk way.

"Eryck…" Saran called out.

"Let him be, Saran. We have much to discuss and he needs time."

Nana was speaking to Saran, but she was looking at the Massive Tree instead, as if it held answers to the questions of the world… like it was a living spirit that could speak to her.

"Nana, I'm soooo sorry…" Saran wanted to make things right. She was upset that Nana knew everything and never told her, but she also knew that she had kept secrets from Nana first. After dropping off a continuously sobbing Yani, the Moorlanders had gone home; and now, Nana and Saran sat alone in the kitchen of the cottage.

"You don't have to apologize, young one." Nana had not called Saran that since she was a small girl, long before the dream states had begun. Nana was calm and Saran could tell that she was ready to talk. "I am the one who should apologize to you. I've kept this secret, and many more, for far too long. Many sleepless nights I wondered if my secrets caused your mother's death. I thought maybe she was the True Dreamer of legend. My mother and my grandmother told me from a young age that I would be the mother of the True Dreamer, and I always assumed it was Allayna." Nana paused to get herself together.

Talking about her daughter was difficult for Naomi Moorlander. "When she died, I knew that she was not the 'one,' and I ultimately began to think the legend was just a myth. I thought that my mother and grandmother had been wrong. I guess I was in denial. I began to look for any sign that the legend wasn't true...instead of looking for signs that it was."

"Nana, did you...do you know what happened on my 12th birthday?"

"I do. I sensed it the night you had the dream. I hadn't had a Dreamer's sense in such a long time. I knew it immediately. I came into the den and saw you sitting at a table talking to Aline. I didn't dare disturb you because I knew of the dangers. You never noticed me there. After that night, I watched you go into various dream states. I wanted to stop you, but I knew I couldn't. I watched you withdraw into the world of dreams.

"I watched you daydream countless times while people would talk to you: lost in your own thoughts. I wanted to stop it, but I didn't know how. The dangers of being a Dreamer have always been known to our family. The Gullivans were our only hope and they all died before your 12th birthday, so their deaths only made me believe that the legend...the curse was untrue. Even though I saw you in a dream state, I thought maybe you would be like me...just a regular Dreamer, not the *True Dreamer*."

"How were the Gullivans the only hope? I thought our family hated the Gullivans?"

"There's a thin line between love and hate, Saran. That's more than an old song and movie, you know? The Gullivans and the Browns are forever tied together. Every few centuries or so, our ancestors would want to break our bond; I grew up in a time when we wanted to be separated from each other. Very rarely were we able to fall in love with other people as long as both families lived on Benaly: we either fell for each other or died alone.

"The Gullivans are a strong race of Dromites that came to Earth long before humankind was formed. Our family, the Browns, believed to be possibly the first humans, are a race of

Dreamers (humans who can connect to each other through our dreams). Dreamers were created to help humans and Dromites keep the world in balance. We are to provide the power of Yin and Yang...benevolence and malevolence. We provide Truth and Honesty to the human race. We keep the stars, sun, and moon in the sky...the water on the Earth so the land can grow and humans can survive. We provide creativity and cultivation.

As we continued to assimilate with normal humans, we became selfish and many of our ancestors on both sides wanted to abandon our responsibilities. Browns wanted to move away from Benaly. Gullivans wanted to live like humans. My mother was one who moved. She brought me here for vacations, but I never wanted to be part of this heritage. I eventually hated to even come to Benaly. And before Papi started working on the cottage I did stay away...for many years I stayed away."

"But what did staying away do, Nana? I mean you found the love of your life here...you met Papi! You had mom. You have me."

Nana looked exhausted. She looked tired like she did the day the Gullivans returned. She looked aged.

"By leaving the island...raising our children off the island like I was raised and how I raised your mother...how I raised you even... well, we weren't able to fine tune our dreaming powers. Many of us didn't even learn all of the energy meditations that allowed us to help other humans. We lost our values. We never learned our true skills.

"We began to keep secrets from each other and lie to one another. I wasn't able to teach your mother or you what to do if you ever started to have dream states and demonstrate the stronger dream powers like what you did today." Saran looked to the ground when her grandmother said this. She felt such horrific pain and humiliation from what she had done to Nana.

But Nana didn't stop. She didn't even sound angry when she recalled Saran's actions. She continued speaking, "I honestly didn't think that you would have powers...your mother never did. I should've known when we returned here, that you could eventually begin to have dream states and possibly exhibit powers. Benaly is a conduit to Drome through the Massive Tree; it helps our people stay connected to Drome. So, I should have known..." Nana looked down. She had started to fidget with her fingers. Saran had never seen her do this before. But as she looked down, she continued, sharing like she had never shared before.

"Never...I mean never in my wildest dreams did I *really* believe that you would be the True Dreamer; I didn't want to believe it. And when it happened, I didn't know what to do, so I just observed. I began to enter my *own* dream states again to see if the ancestors would provide me with knowledge, but they said that you had a Warrior...that it wasn't my place...that I'd given up the right to be involved. I thought my dreams were right, so I stood by and watched. I couldn't figure out how you could have a warrior with all of the Gullivans dead. I didn't really know about Anya, Everett Gullivan's sister, or the child she carried. I'd heard rumors, but we all assumed she was dead and thus shouldn't be spoken of out of respect. I believe now, that she took her child to Drome. She raised him there. Pherron must be her grandchild, like you are mine. It is the only explanation for your connection to Pherron Black and the love you feel for him. He *is* your Dream Warrior."

"Nana, this morning...I..." Saran felt such devastating guilt.

"Say no more, young one. You didn't mean to do it. I have talked to Papi and he sort of understands. But there is more to this, Saran. So much more..." Nana looked weary. Saran began to worry for her grandmother's health for the first time in her life.

Nana was then interrupted by a knock at the door. Saran looked at Nana realizing that it had gotten really late and wondered who would be coming by at this time. It must be Eryck or Yani coming to check on Saran. She got up to answer the door, but Nana stopped her. Naomi Moorlander slowly rose to her feet and opened the door.

"I'm glad you got my message. Thank you for coming. It is time." Nana revealed two men standing in the door: Pherron Black and an elderly man in a deep purple, hooded robe. Saran could not see his face, but she felt like he was familiar somehow. Pherron smiled at Saran and she tried to return it.

"Saran, you must be trained. You must learn to be the True Dreamer. And..." Nana had tears in her eyes. She was struggling to say the words that needed to be said. "You cannot do it here on Earth. You must travel to Drome and learn the Dromite ways. You must learn to control your powers so that you can save humankind from impending doom." Nana said the words quickly as if saying them faster would make the painful truth of them hurt less.

"I don't understand." Saran looked from Pherron to her grandmother.

"Saran, this is my uncle, Everett Gullivan." Saran gasped with this revelation. Everett Gullivan was supposed to be dead. He was supposedly killed in the fire, Saran thought. Pherron continued, "He is a master Dromite. He trained my mother to help her ascend as Queen to the throne of Drome. He then trained me as the prince of Drome. We can train you, but we cannot do it on Earth. You will have to leave here."

"I-don't-understand!" Saran felt a hollow feeling in her stomach and her brand began to burn.

"Sweetheart, you will have to be placed in a deep slumber at the base of the Massive Tree. We will bury you there to preserve your life force, but to the world you will have to die." Nana began to describe the process that would be needed for Saran to go to Drome and stay there without a life force to keep her tethered to Earth as Pherron had been providing earlier that day. Her body could then materialize between Drome and Earth at her command once she was properly trained. She would be the only human capable of this.

"But...what about school? What about Yani and Eryck?" Saran realized that she was beginning to cry. She had wanted to show the world what she could do. She had wanted to stop hiding. And now, she had to die?!? For real? This was not what she wanted. This was the exact opposite of what she wanted!

"They cannot know. Eryck may have powers of his own, but they haven't manifested. And Yani, well, she can never know about the Dreamers or the Dromites. We are meant to protect humans, save humans, but we can't do that if they know about us. Human nature cannot handle what we are." Nana tried to explain, but Saran wouldn't accept it.

"No! I can't leave them. I have to at least tell them the truth. They have to know that Pherron is not bad. They have to know that I am ok."

Pherron looked at Saran as if she were the only person in the room. He came to her and took her hand. She looked at him...at her grandmother...at the man who had returned from the dead. She began to cry and her arm began to throb. Pherron held her at her wrist and the pain subsided, he entered her mind: *I will never hurt you or leave you. I will keep you safe from all harm. I will teach you. And when you are ready, we will return to this place. I will bring you back to your loved ones. This Truth I give to you from my heart and my soul.*

In a deep voice, the silent, robed man spoke to her. He sounded so wise and comforting, like Pherron when he spoke to her in her mind. "Oh, Saran Moorlander, daughter of Allayna Moorlander, daughter of the Brown clan, great True Dreamer of Earth. You have been chosen to save a great race of people. You are stronger than anyone of this world or the next. Do you love this Eryck and Yanieyl?"

Through tears Saran replied, "More than you could know."

"Then you must do this, dear child. The water is still on Earth, but it is nearly gone. Soon the plant life will wither and die. Humans cannot survive without them both. Your

Eryck...your Yanieyl will not survive without water...without food. But they will not accept us taking you away. You must see this to be true?" He pulled his hood back to reveal eyes that were pure white absent a pupil or iris. She wondered how he could see, but he appeared to be looking directly into her soul. As he looked at her, she knew the truth of his words. She felt it.

"And Papi, what will you tell him?" Saran looked at Nana.

"He already knows. I explained *everything* to him. He had long suspected that there was more to our family. He had heard many rumors from people on the island when he would come to repair the cottage. Plus, in the afterlife, Allayna has visited him in his dreams many times. He told me today when you...when the accident happened. He never said anything before because he thought I wouldn't believe him. It was the only thing that helped him understand everything today."

Nana took Saran's hand while Pherron stood protectively next to her. "I would not let them take you if I didn't know it was the right thing to do. You have to know that."

Nana looked from Pherron to Everett and said, "We will begin at dawn."

Saran nodded agreement, but she didn't say anything more. She walked upstairs to her loft without speaking to any of them. Pherron went to follow her, but Nana stopped him. "She needs time to process this and time is what she doesn't have. You...you have an eternity with her." He looked at Nana and nodded. Pherron moved to the door and left with Everett, the man who was supposed to have died in a fire-the master Dromite.

Once upstairs, Saran took out paper and a pen. She began to write. She wrote to her friends with hope that they would find the letter after her mysterious disappearance. She would not leave them to grieve without knowing of her love for them.

Dear Eryck and Yani,

If you find this letter, it means that I am gone. I wish that I had time to tell you everything. I wish I could be here to show you what I can do. I wish I had never kept secrets from you. Right now, you are grieving for me, but I will return. You both are my best friends. Please take care of each other. Do not fight. Love each other as you have loved me. I promise to come back. I will come back to you...in your dreams. Look for me there!

With love,
Saran, your sister and friend forever!

Saran rolled the letter up and placed it in the water bottle she used daily. She hid the bottle under her bed below the floorboards. She hoped that one-day Yani would look for something, anything to remind her of Saran, and she would find it there. After writing the letter, she looked out the window and realized that dawn was soon coming. She packed a bag and went downstairs.

Nana stopped Saran before she got to the bottom step. "You won't need a bag, Saran. I have a gown for you to wear. It is a ceremonial garment for Dreamers. It was the gown of my great-grandmother, Abigail Brown: a great dream interpreter. I am honored to give it to you now."

Saran changed clothes and readied herself for the experience.

When they arrived at the Massive Tree, Pherron and Everett were waiting for them.

"Are you ready, my child?" Everett spoke calmly to Saran. She saw a large box at the base of the tree. It was big enough to hold two people and looked similar to a coffin and a little like a bed. It was lined with what looked like fluffy cotton. Pherron took her hand and escorted her to the box.

"We will sleep here," he said to Saran.

"Inside this box?!? It's a coffin!" Saran began to get nervous, but Pherron circled his wrist and she instantly felt better.

"It's not a coffin. It is a place to keep our bodies preserved for our return, but it also allows our bodies to materialize on Drome." Pherron reassured Saran. They lay down side by side, hands joined together. "I'll see you on the other side," Pherron turned to the side and gave her his cocky smile and kissed her gently.

"Ję ki wọn ala. Ję ki wọn wa ni dabo. Ję ki wọn pada ni akoko, pese sile fun ogun." Everett began to chant these words as Pherron and Saran lay still in the box. Soon, Saran began to feel an overwhelming need to sleep. As her eyelids drew heavy, the last thing she saw was Nana reaching for Everett's hand as the lid was shut on the coffin-bed.

Saran heard her grandmother join Everett:

Ję ki wọn ala. Ję ki wọn wa ni dabo. Ję ki wọn pada ni akoko, pese sile fun ogun.
Ję ki wọn ala. Ję ki wọn wa ni dabo. Ję ki wọn pada ni akoko, pese sile fun ogun.

Let them dream. Let them be preserved. Let them return in time, prepared for battle.

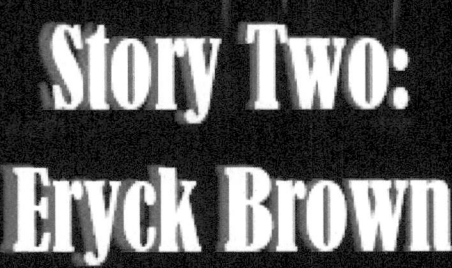

Story Two:
Eryck Brown

A TRUE DREAMER'S LOSS

THE RETURN

Inside her, a baby was growing. She had never felt such joy. From the moment Saran Moorlander died, Yanieyl Starwell had felt mostly emptiness and sadness. Nothing was the same after Saran left except her relationship with Eryck Brown. He became her world. They never fought again; they never dated other people. They never had to make-up because they never broke up again. Everything was about them because they were all each other had. Saran had always been the glue that held them together; her death merely strengthened that bond.

Their senior year of high school had started off crazy with the arrival of Pherron Black and it never got better. Only a few months after school started, Saran had disappeared and so did Pherron Black. Eryck had blamed himself. Naomi and Roderick Moorlander, Saran's grandparents, had moved away suspiciously from Benaly Island. And Yanieyl, she had tried to keep it together as best as possible. They graduated with only each other for support.

After high school, Eryck and Yanieyl moved on to college together in New Charleston, SC only a few miles from Benaly so that they could check on their family as well as keep up the Moorlander cottage. Eryck kept in touch with Naomi and Roderick, but Yanieyl had found it difficult to maintain the relationship with the couple she had known as Nana and Papi. She thought that the elderly couple knew more about Saran's disappearance than they had said and she couldn't bring herself to forgive them. Sometimes, she even doubted Eryck's honesty about the matter, but she wouldn't say anything to him about it: she couldn't afford to lose him too.

Following their fall college graduation ceremony, they checked on the cottage as they had done every year for five years. Afterwards, they decided to return to the Massive Tree. There was no longer a beach there; all of the water had depleted going out sixty miles beyond the original shoreline. In fact, Benaly was no longer considered an island at all. Benaly River was no longer a river. And the mainland was just land.

Benaly was simply a rundown town. People had moved outward as the water depleted, attempting to chase the ocean; and the land was expensive going towards the water, so only the wealthy lived near the new beach. Those without money had to stay in Benaly or move even further inland.

It had been five years to the day since they had last come to the Massive Tree; the last time they saw Saran Moorlander alive. There was a heavy pain on Yanieyl's heart as they drove up to what used to be a beautiful beach.

When they arrived at the tree, Eryck had arranged a candlelit dinner. There was a table there with beautiful linen and china plates: Yanieyl knew they had belonged to his mother. As the sun set, Eryck took Yanieyl's hand in his and pledged his life to Yanieyl asking her to marry him. That was the first day that Yanieyl felt joy in her life again. Eryck spent every day since then making sure Yanieyl had a reason to smile.

Now, several years after being married, Yanieyl and Eryck were leaving the doctor's office where they had seen their baby move on the ultrasound monitor for the first time. They were so excited, but Yanieyl had been having strange dreams throughout her first trimester and they had begun to increase; so, her excitement was clouded by the dreams. Dreams of her baby...dreams of Saran...dreams of Naomi and a hooded man at the Massive Tree. She didn't want to alarm Eryck, but in the past few days she'd even started to have an intense longing to go back to Benaly.

"Bae, I think we should go check on the cottage. We haven't been in a while." Yanieyl told Eryck as they drove back to their townhouse in downtown New Charleston. Like most urban cities, families lived in townhouses and apartments that sat above needed businesses and restaurants. No longer were there suburban areas where homes sat on acres of land or single-family homes in neighborhoods. Everyone was pushed into the cities as the water depleted. Mass dehydration had wiped out entire cities. Trees, grass, and majority of the land on the planet was dying at a rapid pace and people were flocking to the areas that had at one-time bordered oceans, lakes, and rivers.

Eryck looked at Yanieyl with shock. "What brought that about? I usually have to drag you kicking and screaming back to Benaly. Are you ok?"

"Well, I think that I want to check on the house. I have a feeling in my gut that we need to go back."

Yanieyl couldn't explain the dreams and she didn't want to sound crazy, but deep down she felt an extreme urgency to return to the island...to the cottage specifically. "Well, I'll call Nana and Papi to let them know that we are going."

"Ok, great. Can we go tomorrow?" Yanieyl said urgently. Eryck couldn't help but notice. He replied to his wife, "Um...yeah... We can. Are you *sure* you're ok?"

"Yeah, I'm fine. I just...I just really want to go." With that, Eryck let it go. He had gotten used to Yanieyl's mood swings since Saran's death... and now the pregnancy, so he just chalked this weird request up to the baby.

Eryck called his great-aunt, Naomi Moorlander. The phone rang and rang, but eventually the voice mail came on. He tried several times that night but never got an answer which was really strange for the Moorlanders; they usually always answered his calls.

The next morning, Eryck woke to his wife sobbing. "Yani, what's wrong?"

"I don't know. I had the worst dream that Nana was dead. Did you ever get in touch with them?"

"No, I didn't get to talk to them but I'll call them right now. Yani, don't cry. I'm sure it's just a dream." Yanieyl hadn't called Naomi by "Nana" since Saran had died. Eryck noticed that too and was now even more concerned about his wife. Many people had told him that pregnant women would act crazy and irrational, but he felt like the past two days were a little bit passed regular pregnancy moods.

He had Yanieyl lie down on the bed and he went into the bathroom to try calling Nana again. This time, a somber sounding Papi answered the phone. "Hel...Hel-lo."

"Hey...Papi...This is Eryck. I've been calling you all night. Is...Is everything ok?"

"No...no, Eryck, everything is *not* ok. Nana passed away last night." Eryck gasped and pulled the bathroom door in, hoping that Yanieyl wouldn't notice. "I'm gathering up everything to return to the island. She will be buried near the Massive Tree in two days. I'm so sorry, son. I know this will be hard for you. I'm going to have to let you go; I need to make more calls. Will you and Yani be able to come for the service?"

"We wouldn't miss it, Papi! We're going to head to the island now and prepare the cottage for you. That's why I was calling: to ask if it would be ok to go there." Eryck hesitated, but continued on. "Does the rest of the family know?"

"No, you are the first person I have talked to. I need to call your mom and the rest of the clan. Many preparations need to be made and I know that they will want to hold a 'family' ceremony for her."

Papi sounded strained. Eryck didn't know Papi before Nana, but they had been together since they were teenagers and he could only imagine the pain Papi was going through. Eryck couldn't even fathom what he would do if something happened to Yanieyl.

As Eryck turned around, he saw Yanieyl standing in the doorway of the bathroom. He knew instantly that she had overheard everything.

"She's...she's gone, huh?" Yanieyl stuttered the words out. "I...was so horrible...so mean to them. I blamed them for Saran. I blamed her. I wasted all that time and I never got to tell her that I really loved her. That she was like *my* grandmother. That..." Yanieyl sunk to the floor and sobbed while Eryck held her in his arms.

"Yani, baby, it's going to be ok. Nana knew that you loved her, Papi too. They understood the love we both had for Saran. I promise, she knew. But right now, we have to go. We have to get the house ready." Eryck tried his hardest to comfort his wife and he prepared his heart for this new loss: the loss of his great-aunt who had helped raise him–*his* Nana.

Several hours later, Yanieyl and Eryck were driving to the cottage. Though the rest of Benaly was run down and partially abandoned, the Brown's cottage was still beautiful, like life still sprang from it. As they walked into the home, Yanieyl took a deep breath. Every time she came there, it smelled the same: like Nana's cooking and Saran's oils. She always expected that smell to fade after all these years, but it never did. She looked up to the loft that she had spent so much of her childhood in: playing with toys, talking about boys (mostly Eryck), sharing secrets, helping Saran find out about her mysterious family. All of her memories connected back to the Moorlanders and this house.

Though they had come to the house to check on it a few times since high school, Yanieyl had never brought herself to go up to the loft. She guessed that everything would still be the same. Nana and Papi had taken very little with them when they left. They said that they would come back, but they never did. Eryck made the house his responsibility. Yanieyl assumed that Eryck came back more often than he said, but she never wanted to know that truth and so she never put him in the position to have to tell her. That was their life now: secrets and half-truths in the midst of impenetrable love.

Slowly, Yanieyl walked towards the steps. She was apprehensive about going into Saran's room, but she felt drawn to it as she had felt drawn to the island just a day ago. As she came up the steps, she noticed a floorboard under Saran's bed that seemed to be loose or lifted. She knew Saran had a habit of hiding things. Saran wanted the house to be like a treasure chest for generations after her. She always thought that since the Browns were such a mystery, she would give her own children something to find and cherish.

Yanieyl sat on the bed and thought about the floorboard under her. What did Saran leave for future generations? Jewelry? Her oils? Her diary?!? Oh, if Saran left that diary, it would be the best read!

Yanieyl bent on her knees, careful not to disturb her growing belly. She reached under for the floorboard and opened it. Sure enough, there was a box and Saran's favorite water bottle. She pulled the box out first. When she opened it, she was surprised to see pictures of all three of them from kindergarten through high school: Saran, Yanieyl, and Eryck. They had been together for so long.

Yanieyl felt the tears beginning to form in her eyes. She continued to look through the box; she found so many items from their childhood: the smooth green stone they'd found at the Massive Tree when they were 13, the ticket to the fair when they were 8 years old (that was the first time that Eryck had ever kissed Yanieyl), and finally, Saran's mother's favorite earrings. Yanieyl finally let the tears fall as she reminisced about her life with her best friend and sister.

Lastly, Yanieyl picked up the water bottle. She knew instantly that she would keep the bottle. Once the drought began and people began to store and ration water, Saran had carried that bottle with her everywhere.

Inside the bottle was a small piece of paper. Yanieyl pulled out the paper and began to read:

Dear Eryck and Yani,

If you find this letter, it means that I am gone. I wish that I had time to tell you everything. I wish I could be here to show you what I can do. I wish I had never kept secrets from you. Right now, you are grieving for me, but I will return. You both are my best friends. Please take care of each other. Do not fight. Love each other as you have loved me. I promise to come back. I will come back to you...in your dreams. Look for me there!

With love,
Saran, your sister and friend forever!

"Eryck, come up here! Right-Now!" Yanieyl was frantic. Eric ran up the stairs, frightened that something was wrong with the baby.

"What's wrong? Are you ok? Is it the baby?!?" Eryck looked at his wife sitting on Saran's bed. There were pictures and items strewn all over the bed and Yanieyl was holding a small piece of paper; her hands were trembling. "What do you have in your hand?"

Yanieyl merely held the paper up. She sat in shock: tears running down her eyes, but she never made a sound.

"Eryck, she knew. She said she's coming back. She said she would come in our dreams...she...Bae," Yanieyl realized that she had to tell Eryck about the dreams now. "I have...I have something to tell you."

After Eryck read the letter, he dropped down on the bed beside Yanieyl never taking his eyes off the rolled up paper. Slowly he responded, "I have something to tell you, too."

They both looked at each other and said simultaneously: "I've been keeping secrets from you!" They both realized what they had said and looked down in shame.

Eryck started, "Yani, when Saran died...or left," he kept looking at the letter "...or whatever, I didn't know what to do. It was *my* fault. I pushed her, I made her run to *him*, and I never even listened to her." Eryck was beginning to cry. In all of their life, the only time she had seen him cry was when it was about Saran.

"I know...I know you felt like it was your fault, but you couldn't stop *anything* that was happening. Pherron did something to her. We both knew that. But even afterwards...I...I didn't believe...I had..." Yani tried to comfort Eryck.

"Yani, just hold on. There's more." Eryck paused, but not long enough for Yanieyl to stop him. "After Saran left, something happened that I didn't tell you. That night...the night she left... I went home and talked to my mom and she said that everything would be ok. She said that I shouldn't be mad and that everything would become clear in time."

"What do you mean?" Yanieyl forgot all of *her* secrets and began to wonder what Eryck had been keeping. She knew that he didn't tell her everything and she had accepted that; but she never thought that he would keep anything from her that pertained to Saran or Saran's disappearance.

"I started having these...dreams. They started the night Saran disappeared. They were..." Eryck wasn't sure how to explain this to Yanieyl, "they were intense. They...I...I talked directly to my ancestors in the dreams. They told me things. And my parents..."

"Wait a minute, you had *dreams* where you were talking to people from your family? What type of..." Yanieyl began to stand up.

Eryck stopped her, "please...please let me finish."

She looked at this man that she had known her entire life: This man that loved her and cared for her. She felt like her world was being undone. Saran had left a note saying that she *knew* she was leaving and she was planning to come back...in their dreams. And sure enough, Yanieyl had been having dreams of Saran for months since she had gotten pregnant. And now...now, Eryck was saying that he had been having these dreams for all the years they'd been together.

"Baby, please listen. My family...we...well, my family has the ability to connect to each other in our dreams. I was told that I couldn't tell you...that I had to keep this secret for *our* safety. But I also didn't think that my dreams had anything to do with Saran's disappearance... I mean they're *dreams*. Not real. And I never had one single dream about Saran...I promise you!" Eryck knelt in front of Yanieyl and peered into her eyes. He wanted her to understand and forgive him. Yani could not stop herself.

"Eryck, I can't believe you wouldn't at least tell me. I've been going through so much for the past few months because I thought I was going crazy. I've had dreams of Saran lately...Dreams where she talks to me and tells me that she is happy and that she will come home to us. And last night, I dreamed that Nana was dead. I saw her breathe her last breath! What does all this mean?!? Is Saran coming back or not?!?"

Yanieyl had maintained her composure as long as she could. She was crying hysterically and Eryck didn't know what to say or do, so he simply held her in his arms.

"Yanieyl, let's go to the Massive Tree. Let's talk about it there, where we are closest to Saran. No more secrets. No lies. And then, we'll ask my mother about the letter. We'll find out about everything."

He reached for Yanieyl's face and cupped it in his hands. He slowly kissed her and she felt the rightness of what he had said. They needed to go to the Tree. They would be able to sort everything out then.

At the Massive Tree, they were surprised to see two people in dark, hooded robes: one seemingly tall, the other short with a slight slump. Eryck and Yanieyl exchanged a look that said they would hold back to see who was there. As they observed the two people, they noticed that they had shovels in their hands. Eryck whispered to Yanieyl, "They don't look like grave diggers." Yanieyl shushed him, but nodded in agreement. She motioned for them to move closer, and they did.

They moved behind a dumpster that had been left near the tree (things had surely changed over the years). They could hear the voices of the two people.

The taller person, a woman's voice, began to talk, "Everett, we must remove them. Now that Naomi has gone on, they need to come back. Naomi never knew her purpose...she never cared; but her death has grave implications for this planet. Naomi's funeral will bring many Dreamers and Warriors from far and wide... many that abandoned our ways. And some that aren't even part of our bloodlines." Eryck and Yanieyl looked at each other quizzically. Eryck lifted his finger to his nose to signal quiet.

The shorter person began to speak revealing an elderly man's voice, "Anya, we don't know if they have finished the training yet. To remove them too early could be catastrophic."

"And if some local tourists discover the portal? What do we do then? I allowed them to go. I allowed him to hold the throne in my absence so I could come back here since you sent them against my wishes." The woman touched her temples in frustration. "I understand your role as guardian and elder to the throne, but times have changed and I believe it is just as dangerous to leave them there than to revive them." The woman sounded authoritative but apprehensive, as if she wanted the old man to agree with her, not just merely let her have her own way; she wanted approval.

The old man gave in, "Roderick will be here tonight. We can make a decision then. Naomi has given him knowledge, power, and access to our world. She has shared all of our traditions with him...at least those within her knowledge. We will discuss it with him since it pertains to *his* granddaughter and then we'll come back at dusk." The two turned and left without noticing Eryck or Yanieyl, who immediately went back to their car to discuss what happened.

"What the heck was that?!?" Yanieyl exclaimed as soon as they were in the car.

"I have no clue! But, believe it or not, I know what Dreamers are, or at least who the Dreamers are. But the crazy thing is that they're talking about Saran!" Eryck was looking intensely at the road laid before him wanting nothing more than to have remembered the stories Nana had told Saran and him when they were small.

She always told of a world of dreams, where dreams could provide knowledge and power. He always considered them fairy tales...something to put them to sleep, but now with everything they had seen...everything he had witnessed in his own dreams, he was no longer sure about anything at all.

"Let's go to my mom's. I'm sure she'll have answers. One thing's for sure, we *will* be back at the Massive Tree... *before* dusk. There's no way we're missing whatever it is they plan on doing." Yanieyl looked at her husband and silently agreed.

THE REVELATION

"How much have you told Yanieyl?" Eryck's mother, Kyia Brown, looked terrified as she asked her son about his wife.

"Mom, at this point, I've told her everything I know. Nana is gone and Yani is my wife! I'm done keeping secrets from her." Eryck never understood the secrets and mysteries of his family. As young children, it was one of the many things he and Saran had had in common. They had searched every family home they'd ever entered. They looked for trinkets and letters. They looked for pictures...not to see the people in them, but to look in the background of the pictures for any clue to their heritage. They hid around corners to observe the things their parents and grandparents concealed when they spoke in hushed tones or when they told abbreviated versions of stories that clearly had details missing. And though he loved his mother and he knew that she loved Yanieyl, Kyia had acted strange towards Yani from the moment they got married though she had never acted that way before.

"I just don't think she is ready for all of this. I don't even know if you are. There is so much *involved* in learning about your family. It's not like we can sit down, have a drink, and discuss it. There are books to be read, secrets to be told, rituals to perform...some of which are very unpleasant to say the least." Kyia's hands had begun to shake and Eryck noticed that she was fidgeting with the hem of her skirt to hide her trembling anxiety. It made him uneasy to think that any secret could rattle or shake his steadfast mother.

"I shouldn't have to be the one to tell you about this. Your father..." Kyia stopped. She rarely discussed her deceased husband or his parents. Eryck Brown, Sr. had died soon after she had given birth to her only son. His parents died one year later, leaving Kyia to raise young Eryck alone; and at times, she seemed bitter about this. Naomi Moorlander, however, had stepped up for the Brown family and helped her raise him. *She* was supposed to be the one to help Eryck understand all this. Naomi wasn't supposed to leave Benaly and leave Kyia to try to explain things. It wasn't until Eryck turned 18 years old that Kyia was truly let in on the secrets of the Brown family and the world of dreams; and when she did, it had rocked her world. So many things changed for her at once.

She loved Yanieyl Starwell, the girl who had captivated her son at first sight. Yani had always been the daughter she never had. Though Saran and Eryck were always close, Yani was an outsider like she had been at one time which made Kyia and Yani's bond even stronger. Kyia had known nothing about her family growing up. She was adopted around the age of twelve by a rather distant and cold, older couple who died soon after she graduated from high school. She had no memories of anything before being adopted which was always odd. And, sometimes, she missed her adoptive family... but Yani had made her feel like she had family other than the mysterious Browns.

To invite Yani into the wonders, as well as the horrors, of Dreamers and their customs was the very last thing Kyia had ever wanted for her daughter-in-law.

"Your father never told me anything because of the dangers." Eryck could hear the anger in her voice, but there was something else there. Something that felt like she was still holding back...even now.

"You keep talking about dangers, but you aren't telling me anything! Right now, my wife, the woman I have loved since I was a little kid, is upstairs reliving the disappearance of her best friend...*our* best friend. I've had to lie to her and keep secrets from her that I don't even understand. I have dreams where people talk to me like they're in my room! And now...now, Yani is having crazy dreams. She knew that Nana had died when she woke up this morning. It's happening to her! And all you can do is give me vague responses. It's not fair! So just tell me what's happening!"

Kyia took a deep breath and pushed her skirt down one final time. "When you were six years old, I came into your room and you...you were literally floating in the air. You were saying the same words over and over, and I couldn't understand you...because you weren't speaking English."

Kyia stopped to assess her son...to look into his eyes to see if there was apprehension or disbelief, but he sat calmly, listening like everything she'd just said was normal. She judged her words carefully and continued, "I tried to touch you, but as I reached for you I felt an electric shock and was pushed backwards. I tried several times before I finally freaked out. I called Naomi and she rushed over. I remember thinking in the middle of all that craziness that it was odd that she came alone...without Papi.

"When she went into your room, she cried silent tears. She didn't make a sound. She said that she wondered if you would be a Dreamer and that this was a sign that you were a Principal Dreamer, but also a sign that you had Warrior blood in you too. Of course, I had no clue what she was talking about. She came to me and placed her hand on my forehead and said some words: *Orun, omo[1].* I woke up three days later in my bed. I didn't know where I was and I didn't remember what happened to you, but I remembered those three words. Orun, omo." Kyia stopped talking and stared at a picture on the piano: a picture of Eryck's father.

Eryck looked at his mother and wondered what she was thinking... What was she so scared to tell him? "Mom, Is there," he wasn't sure if he should interrupt her, "...is there more?"

"Oh...yeah..." She seemed to snap out of a trance, "Well, when I woke up, there was a note from Naomi that she had picked you up and kept you while I was sick. I didn't remember being sick, but I felt different. I asked Naomi many times what happened and she said that I had called sounding delirious, so Papi had taken you to the cottage and she had sat with me for those days. The story never did sit well with me. But nothing strange ever happened again."

"Years later, you woke up one night and were walking around the house. I remember it was around Saran's 12th birthday because you had been wanting to go pick something out for her days before. That night, you were talking to someone, but no one was there. When I woke you up, you...you just looked at me. You never said one word; you just turned around and went back to bed. Of course, I didn't know what to think. When I told Nana about it, she was as white as a sheet; but she just said you were probably sleep walking. You kept sleep walking for years after that and I would always wake you up. You would go back to bed and never speak about it, so I didn't speak about it. Then your senior year came..."

"Senior year..." Eryck repeated the words with trepidation.

"I know that was the worst year of your life. But nothing about that year was what it seemed. At the time, I didn't know *anything*...I swear to you, I didn't know anything at all! I just

---

[1] Sleep, child.

knew I had a 'sleep walking' son, but I wasn't prepared at all for what was revealed to me that year."

"Yeah, I think we have some idea of how you felt." Eryck hesitated, " Mom, Saran left a note for me and Yani. She talked about dreams and coming back. I know we all thought she died, but what if..."

Eryck hadn't dared say the thought aloud that Saran might still be alive. He never wanted to get his hopes up, but he had never really believed she was dead. Today, he said what he had always hoped and felt was true, "...what if Saran isn't dead? What if she is just gone somewhere? What if...what if she is coming back?"

Kyia stared at her son for several moments before saying the unbelievable, "Eryck...my son...Saran isn't dead."

Glass shattered behind them and at the doorway stood Yanieyl palefaced with blood coming from her hand.

"What-did-you-just-say?" Yanieyl didn't move. She didn't notice the blood flowing from her hand. She stared at Ercyk and Kyia in anticipation of an answer. They said nothing. "ANSWER ME!!!!!" Yanieyl yelled so loud that Kyia jumped.

"Yani, wait a sec..." Eryck moved towards her.

"NOOOO! You wait. What- -did- -you- -just- -say?" Yani's voice came out like a growl. Kyia didn't know what to do or say. She knew what hearing that, in that manner, would do to Yani and hurting Yanieyl was never her intention.

"Yanieyl, I...I didn't mean for you to hear it like that." Kyia tried to sound calm. She was typically a strong woman who had suffered many losses and heartaches and had survived, but everything she knew about the Brown family had taken its toll on her stability over the past few years.

"You didn't mean for me to hear it like that or you didn't mean for me to hear it all?!? Saran and Eryck have been my best friends and family for my entire life. I have always known that there were secrets in the family. But you...you were *my* family.

Me and you, thick and thin. How could you ever keep something like this from me...or even Ercyk?!?"

"How about the two of you come sit down? I'll tell you everything that I know." She took Yanieyl by the hand...calmly...delicately. She bandaged her wound and took her to the sitting room.

Eryck and Yanieyl listened to Kyia tell the story of their senior year and how she was introduced to the world of dreams:

"Your senior year was hard for everyone. Eryck, I just told you how you started sleep walking when you were six. I watched you do this for many years and it was always harmless. But your senior year, everything changed. When Pherron Black showed up, your whole demeanor changed...he brought out an 'anger' in you that I'd never seen. I thought that it was because Saran had finally met someone and you were being overprotective, but of course within weeks they were gone. The day that she...died. Well, the first time she died you came home so upset that you didn't notice that there was a mark on the back of your neck...like a brand...but Naomi noticed. The next day, she asked me about it. I told her that I saw it and it looked like a small cloud with three lightning bolts going through it. I could tell she knew what it was, but she didn't say anything else. That was the first day I really *felt* like she wasn't being totally honest with me."

Eryck felt the back of his neck. The brand was still there. He remembered that his neck had burned the day that Saran met Pherron Black. Now that he thought about it, it had burned when they were at the tree the last time he had seen Saran. He hadn't thought about that mark since then; now he wondered why he hadn't.

"That last day that you guys were with Saran, I went to the cottage. Rod was there, but Naomi was gone. He said that she had gone to take care of some business...but he looked shaken up. I asked him if everything was ok, and he just said that he hoped so. By the time I got back, you were already home saying Pherron Black had done something to Saran. You were in a murderous rage. I gave you tea, do you remember?" Eryck shook his head as he remembered that night.

"Well, the tea had a sedative in it. I wanted you to sleep. At first, I just wanted you to rest. You'd had a rough week and you honestly were scaring me with your angry, erratic behavior; I really just wanted you to have some form of peace. You were sleeping so hard that I decided to go back to the cottage to talk to Naomi about everything that was going on... to force her to be truthful," Kyia stopped. She knew that once she started this, there was no going back.

"When I started to pull up to the cottage I noticed a black sedan pulling out, so I decided not to even pull in to the driveway at all. Something in me told me to follow the car, and I did. I followed it to the Massive Tree. When I got to the tree Pherron Black was standing there and a man that I had seen before. It had been many years, but I knew who he was. It was Everett Gullivan." Eryck and Yani exchanged knowing glances.

"He was supposed to be dead but he was standing right there. The black car door opened and Naomi and Saran got out of the car. I remember thinking how strange it was for them to be out so late without Rod. Saran ran to Pherron and they hugged each other like they had known each other for years when I knew it had only been a few weeks or so. What really blew my mind was when Naomi greeted and hugged Everett Gullivan. I mean every-single-person on Benaly knows about the Brown/Gullivan feud. Every one! And there they were, hugging like old friends. Pherron motioned to some men who were standing near the tree and they pulled a large truck up to the tree. I didn't see it at first, but there was a huge hole in the ground at the base of the tree. The men pulled out a box the size of a queen-size bed and lowered it into the hole in the ground."

Kyia took a moment to breathe. Even replaying the events in her mind was exhausting. She couldn't imagine what it sounded like to her only son. "I watched them as Pherron and Saran took each other's hands and stepped into the box and lay down. I was so terrified. Naomi and Everett joined hands and began to chant. As they did, they closed the box, sealed it shut, and buried it below the tree."

"Stop!" Yanieyl had heard enough. "Are you telling me that they buried my best friend alive?!?"

"No, Yani...I'm telling you that your best friend is still alive and that she *chose* to do this."

"Do *this*? Do what?!?" Eryck was now feeling a lot like his wife. He felt hurt, betrayed, scared, confused...so many emotions at one time. He looked at Yanieyl and took her by the hand. They could do anything together. They needed to remain together, but she pulled her hand free. Eryck looked at his wounded wife and wondered about the damage the truth, or maybe the lies, would have on their relationship.

"Saran and Pherron have been frozen in a type of sleep state. This state allowed Saran's human mind and body to be preserved for eternity while she materializes in the World of Drome.

"You know what...I'm good. Eryck, you've lied to me! Kyia, you too. I think both of you are crazy. I thought I knew *you*." Yanieyl looked at Eryck and stood up to leave.

"Yanieyl Starwell, sit- - down!" The strong woman Eryck had always known emerged. Kyia stood up and looked at Yanieyl as only a mother could, and Yani sat down.

"Everything is not always black and white! You children have snooped all over this island looking for answers. Well, here you go! Hell, I never wanted to know all this! I never wanted to be a part of this...not ever!!! You are not the only ones who lost someone. I never had anyone before all this and the few people I loved died too damn early! They left me here with all..." she circled the room and air, "...THIS! They let me go through this without ever thinking whether I was strong enough to handle the truth and that I would *have to* handle it at some point anyway. And then they left and let it fall down on me like an avalanche. So, you *will* sit down and you *will* listen!"

Eryck reached for his wife's hand again; this time she gave it to him and she squeezed tight. Kyia continued to explain what happened so many years before when Saran disappeared.

"After they buried them, it was like I came out of a trance. I ran to the tree screaming. I told them that I was going to call the police and that they were committing murder. The second I got close to them, Naomi looked at me and said, 'Ranti aye re! [2]' As soon as she said it, a rush of memories came to me. The memories from the night when you were six, Eryck. But even more memories. The memories of my parents, my real parents. The memories of horrible deaths and blood. Memories of love and care. Memories of Drome: a world of dreams and warriors. The moment she said those words, I knew exactly what happened to Saran and Pherron, I knew who Pherron was, and I knew who I was. I knew what happened to your father and his parents. And, most importantly, I knew what would happen to you...I knew what *I* had done."

Eryck and Yanieyl were speechless. They didn't know what to say or ask. They were still confused, but now...now Kyia was involved in this and they couldn't be mad at her any longer.

"Guys, your lives will never be the same again. You are bringing a child into a world that you don't even understand. And it's my fault. It's your dad's fault. It's who we are. Eryck, for many years I didn't know anything about my family or myself. The Ayers took me in and they kept me housed and fed. I had no memories of my life before them and they never tried to give me any clues; I'm not even sure if they had clues to give. I

---

[2] Remember your life

wasn't sure if I was born here on Benaly or somewhere else. But when Naomi said those words: 'Ranti aye re,' it meant 'Remember your life' and it allowed to me to remember everything. I am a child of Drome: An ancestor of the Gullivan family. I am not the age that you think I am."

Preparing to tell her story gave Kyia a sense of life-altering reality crashing down around her. She would have to admit things to her son that she never thought she would have to speak of again. The world...the culture that she had run from. She forced herself to tell her story:

"When I was a child, over 500 years ago...or maybe longer...I don't really know anymore...I wanted to escape my destiny. I didn't want to be a Warrior: I wanted to be an independent woman. We were mated at a young age back then and I knew that when I turned twelve on Drome my destiny would begin. I didn't want everything to be chosen for me. I wanted to have a husband of my choosing. I wanted to be free of Drome and Benaly Island. I tried to run away, but my parents found out my plans. They placed me in a dream state for more years than you can understand, but before they did they removed all of my memories.

"Only a few elders knew and they recorded it for future elders. Somehow, I resurfaced, and I wandered Benaly until the Ayers took me in. They never knew anything about me, but Everett Gullivan did. He watched me and made sure that my memories did not come back. He kept me in a modified sleep state: Orun, ọmọ or Sleep, young child. That is why I remembered the words so well when you were six, Eryck. It had been said to me over and over for decades...centuries even."

Eryck and Yanieyl just listened...dumbfounded by the story that unraveled before them. Kyia didn't stop.

"Naomi understood me though. She finally decided to intervene. She had avoided Benaly because of the disagreements between her family and the elders. But when Allayna died, she came back and she exposed what they were doing to me.

Maybe she wouldn't have had she known who I really was. Without Everett taking my memories, I was free to do the things that I wanted to do, or to fall in love with who I wanted. Eventually I fell in love with your dad. I didn't have my past memories, but I could make future ones." Kyia, who hadn't looked at the young couple while she spoke finally made eye contact with her son.

"Of course, I didn't know the repercussions of getting involved with Eryck Brown. See, Eryck wasn't a Principal Dreamer. He didn't have powers to intervene with humans as Principal Dreamers do. That type of power was thought to have flowed through Naomi and her female descendants. The men in the Brown family rarely possessed the powers of Principal Dreamers. By the time I was an adult, there wasn't anyone on Benaly who truly knew who I was or that a relationship between Eryck and I would be bad except Everett."

"Everett had gone into hiding and even Naomi didn't know our true connection...she didn't know I was *born* as a Dromite Warrior. Warriors are not sent to Earth to mate with just *any* Dreamer. Each Warrior has a blood tie to an individual Dreamer's bloodline. Sometimes we have to wait on Drome for what amounts to centuries on Earth before our sworn Dreamer is even born. Because time on Drome moves so slowly compared to time on Earth, children can be born on Drome, trained in Drome, and centuries would have gone by on Earth. When an Earth Dreamer is born, the Dreamer is sent to Earth at a time where their ages would seem similar. But in actuality, Dromites are hundreds, if not thousands, of years older than humans.

"Pherron is Saran's Warrior. He was sent here for her. He is, however, really the son of Anya Gullivan; and he was born on Earth and raised on Drome. He *should* be as old as Allayna would have been. But since he grew up on Drome, he was able to return as a teenager like you guys, though he has lived for many decades more. When Saran returns here, she will still be seventeen while you have been aging all these years."

Yani interrupted with a whisper, "So...she *is* coming back?"

"Yes, Yanieyl, she is coming back. She has an important task. She has to save us all from the destruction of Earth." This was the part that was the hardest to digest. Eryck and Yanieyl looked at each other in disbelief as they learned more about the Dreamer culture.

"So why are we having the dreams too?" Eryck asked.

"Eryck, you are a Principal Dreamer. You shouldn't be, but you are. I shouldn't have been able to have a child by your father; he wasn't *my* Dreamer. And, he was a Dormant Dreamer. He could interpret dreams, but he couldn't commune with the ancestors or intervene with other humans' dreams. We weren't linked in any way, so I definitely shouldn't have been able to have a *Principal Dreamer* by him. I believe when I ran from my destiny, I think I tipped the fates out of balance."

Eryck and Yanieyl looked confused. There was so much to try to understand, and Kyia was rushing through it like everything made total sense. Dad had no powers, Mom had powers, Eryck had powers...just total craziness and confusion. But still they listened.

"Like Saran, your birth was foreseen, Eryck: The Dromite Warrior born of a 'shunned' Warrior and a Dormant Dreamer. Saran is supposed to be the savior of humankind while you are supposed to bring the destruction. The brand on your neck symbolizes how lightning will rain down on Earth destroying it in fire. Because the water will be gone, the lightning will burn everything in its path. And you...you will bring the lightning."

"What?!? Why on Earth would I do such a thing?" Eryck was flabbergasted. "First of all, I love you, Yani, and Saran. Why would I do something that would hurt you?"

"You won't know. The same way you sleep walk and have no memories of it. Dreamers remember sleep states, but with your mixed blood you won't necessarily remember what you do when you are in a dream state."

"I remember the ones I've been having lately! Doesn't that mean this is wrong?" Eryck was trying to grasp this curse on him. He loved his family. He would never do anything that would hurt them. He couldn't understand how anyone would even think him capable of such harm.

"And what about me?" Yani interjected, "Why am I having these dreams?"

"I think your baby is the one having the dreams and you are just receiving them. I don't know if you will still have these dreams after the baby is born. But that baby...that baby is strong to project dreams to you." Kyia speculated this because technically, once a dreamer's bloodline became dormant like her husband's blood was, they were not supposed to produce Principal children ever again. Their entire family lines were the ones who were free to live normal human lives. "Like I said, Eryck is an anomaly and your child will be as well."

"That's assuming I don't bring about the end of the world?" Eryck grumbled under his breath. "Ok so, Yani and I saw two people at the Massive Tree today talking about taking Saran out. It was Everett Gullivan and someone named Anya."

Kyia gasped, "Anya! Are you sure? There is no way Anya would be on Earth!"

"Well, the old man called her Anya. She seemed to be someone important." Yani chimed in.

"Anya is the current ruler of Drome. She should be on Drome with Saran and Pherron." Kyia stated quizzically and somewhat nervously.

"Well, she is here, and she said she wants to raise Saran and Pherron tonight before Naomi's funeral." Yani continued. Eryck was oddly quiet, but Yani knew that he was brewing. She gave his hand a squeeze; she hadn't dared let go of his hand again.

"They can't come back yet! Surely, she isn't completely trained. Dreamers train for decades in Earth time..." Suddenly there was a knock at the door. Kyia looked nervously to the door as Eryck stood to answer it. "No! Don't answer it!" Kyia looked very afraid as she turned to look at the clock; it was nearly 10 o'clock at night.

"Eryck...step away from the door. Take Yanieyl and go. Go as far away from here as you can. I promise I will tell you everything later. Just go. I'll contact you! Under your bed is a door with tunnels leading out of Benaly. Use it to escape. Don't look back. You have to go now!"

Eryck saw the urgency in his mother's eyes as the knock at the door rang out loudly as if someone were actually coming through the door: "Kyialles, Ṣii ilẹkùn, o gbọdọ wa bayi![3]" The voice was powerful. With tears in her eyes, Kyia turned and whispered, "GO- -NOW! I love you, my son and daughter...NEVER forget that! I will contact you. G-O-O-O!"

Without another word, Eryck turned with his wife and followed his mother's instructions. He didn't know that he would never again see his mother alive...at least not in this world.

Once inside the home of Eryck Brown, twelve Warriors stood before Kyia Brown. "Kyialles of the Gullivan tribe. You stand guilty of delivering the curse upon this world. How do you plead?"

Kyia stood proudly with her chin up and her hands outstretched for the shackles that would surely be placed on her arms. "I want to look her in her eyes. Take me to Anya!" She would speak to Anya of Drome. She would speak... to her mother!

---

[3] Open the door, you must come now!

ALL HAIL THE QUEEN

"I can't go any further. I'm tired and I'm hungry. How long before we get to the end of these tunnels?" Yanieyl looked weary from their journey in the tunnels and she knew that Eryck had no more of a clue where they were going than she did. After fleeing Eryck's home, they had said very little to each other. They didn't know *what* to say. They had left his home with more questions than answers and fear running through their blood.

"Eryck, we have to stop!" Yanieyl grabbed Eryck by the arm and stopped him. "Babe, she's going to be ok."

"No, Yani, she isn't. I can feel it. Something bad was about to happen. The knocks on the door weren't from lil' girls selling Girl Scout cookies!"

He started to look around. Suddenly, he looked at Yani anxiously. He quickly sputtered out, "We have to go back!"

"Eryck! You haven't been listening to me. I can't go *anywhere*! I need to stop. I need to rest. I understand what you are feeling, but I am still pregnant. We have to stop." She pleaded with her husband. She tried to get him to look at her, really see her. She moved in front of him and cupped his face in her hand...he leaned into it and kissed her palm. He looked into her eyes and she knew that he saw her then.

"Oh my goodness, Yani! I'm so sorry. I haven't even...I'm so, so sorry. We can rest. I grabbed a few things from the room when we left. Let's find somewhere you can sit down."

The tunnels under Eryck Brown's home were old. They looked to be centuries old. They had no clue where the tunnels lead; they didn't know where they would come out. But his mother had said it would be outside of Benaly. They had been running and walking for over five miles. Eryck knew they lived at least ten miles inside the city limits which meant they still had far to go on foot. He took a moment to look around. The walls were smooth but circular: there wasn't a clearly defined difference between the ceiling, the walls, and the ground. It was old, but it appeared to be well-maintained. They could put a blanket down and rest for a while and still be able to hear if anyone came from either direction.

He ran his fingers along the wall and looked around with his flashlight. In their panic, he hadn't noticed that there were pictures all along the walls. He turned towards the direction they had come and realized that the pictures went back in that direction as well. He looked forward, and the pictures went as far as he could see with the light.

The pictures in front of him seemed to tell a story. There were pictures of men, women, and children. But there were also pictures of land with multiple moons and suns. Animals that looked like nothing he had ever seen in his life. He was drawn to one symbol that lay directly in front of him: a cloud with three lightning bolts running through it just like the brand on his neck. As he continued to stare at the symbol, the bolts seemed to pulsate and flash. As his hand connected to the flashing lightning bolts, the entire tunnel illuminated with light.

"What the heck was that?!?" Yanieyl exclaimed. Fear had settled in her voice again. "Do you think we were followed?"

"No, I just touched this symbol. I think it made the tunnel light up. Look at the wall. I think...I think that this man on the wall is me." Eryck was staring at one figure on the wall and beside the man in the picture was a pregnant woman who looked like Yanieyl. "And...and that's you."

Yanieyl walked over to the wall to see what Eryck was looking at. Sure enough there was a picture of two figures that looked exactly like her and Eryck. She reached out and touched the wall; immediately, the ground began to move.

"What did I do? Oh God! What- - did- -I- -just- - do?" She looked at Eryck and he grabbed her hand. They started to run; but as soon as they took a step, the rumbling stopped instantly.

"Eryck wait! It stopped."

She moved towards the wall again and put her hand to the wall; the rumbling began again.

"Yani, stop! I don't know what is happening but *you* do not need to touch that wall!" Eryck looked nervous as he pulled Yanieyl away from the wall.

Once he felt safe enough for them to sit down, he placed a large, downy blanket on the ground. In his satchel, he pulled out a protein bar and a bottle of water. "Here, eat this. I'm sorry I wasn't thinking before. Everything happened so fast that all I could think about was getting you to safety and then getting away from the danger I left my mother in."

"Kyia's a survivor, Eryck. She'll be ok. She wanted us to be safe. I could see it in her face."

"I know. You're right. I just can't shake the feeling that she is in danger...that we are all in danger."

"Well, apparently that is the one thing we agree on. Who knew our day would go like this? I hate that we can't call Papi and check on him. I know he will wonder where we are."

Yanieyl felt so many emotions. She wanted to be with Papi to tell him how much he and Nana had meant to her. She wanted to apologize for the past few years. She wanted to find out what was going to happen with Saran. She thought about everything and cried out, "What if they bring Saran back and we aren't there? Eryck, our sister is coming back!"

"Yeah, but back to what? Back as who? If Mom is right, she'll be a teenager. Will it even be the same? And all this stuff about Earth's destruction. Some of that has to be real. The water *is* leaving the planet. We don't even have a beach in Benaly anymore. If that part is true, doesn't it mean that the part about me is true too?"

"Eryck, we can't believe that. You're a good man. There's no way you would ever voluntarily hurt any of us. If the story is true, we'll figure it out together like we always do."

"Can we figure this out, Yani? We went to mom's to 'figure this out' and now we are on the run from someone...in tunnels we never knew about...under the city where our best friend is buried with some strange guy..."

Eryck had exhausted himself just trying to get it all out. "We know more *and* less than before we went to see her. And now...Mom could be dead, Yani!"

"Eryck, everything is crazy right now. I won't lie. I'm scared, but I know that Kyia wanted you...wanted *us* to be safe. And if she's in danger, she knew what that danger was. She knows more than us. Do you realize that your mother just told us that she's hundreds of years old? We have to trust that whatever happened, she was prepared for it. We have to think about us and our baby. We have to figure out what is going on by ourselves for right now. But most importantly, we have to get out of these tunnels." Yani was right and Eryck knew it; so, they sat and rested for a while.

Kyia Brown sat in a dark room. It was small; but it had a bed, a closet, and a dresser with Warrior's clothes in it...clothes that were just her size. She walked around and looked for a way out of the room, or a way in. There were no doors or windows in the room. The warriors who had taken her that night had put her into a sleep state. She wasn't sure when or where she was: on Earth or elsewhere.

She wanted to cry. She had been going through various rituals to bring back *all* of her memories and powers since Naomi had 'awakened' her, but there were times when she would forget things. She knew, however, that Anya would want to punish her. And her punishment would be death.

A small light began to pulsate on the wall to the right of the bed. Slowly, the light grew to the size of a door and a shadow emerged. The light vanished quickly and a table with two chairs materialized beside the bed.

"Hello, Kyialles."

"Hello, Anya."

"Anya? If you aren't going to speak to me in an appropriate familiar tone, refer to me as 'Your Majesty'"

Anya sat down at the table and motioned for Kyia to do the same. Kyia was reluctant but saw no need to fight the inevitable. They both knew that Anya could make her sit.

"I will not refer to you as anything other than Anya. Would you prefer that I call you what I really want? Evil one? Horrible mother? Destroyer of lives?"

"How dare you speak to me like that?!?"

"How dare I? How dare you? Why don't you just kill me? I know that is what you are planning." In a sarcastic and mocking tone, Kyia continued to taunt the Queen, "I have brought about the destruction of your beautiful era. We both know this world will not end, only the humans who reside in it. Dear Mother, are you afraid to lose your puppets?"

"You know nothing of me or my plans! Why do you make me to be the villain? Have I not taken in your True Dreamer, Saran?" Anya tried to sound pleasant as she asked the rhetorical questions, but Kyia heard the annoyance in her voice.

Only one other person on Earth knew the true myth of the True Dreamer. Kyia, Anya, and Everett Gullivan. Aside from them, no other beings on Earth were old enough to remember the original prophecy.

Kyia had not been entirely truthful with her son. She was old...she was extremely old. To be honest, Kyia didn't know how old she was in Earth terms, but she knew it was old...ancient even. She had come and gone from Drome so many times in her lifetime, that she truly did not remember the beginning of her life. And that was her mother's fault...it was Anya's fault.

"Please. You have taken so much from me...too much. But what I do know is that you have waited for Saran for a long time. Maybe Uncle E has forgotten, but that is a memory I still have."

"Do not speak of things you know nothing about!"

"I know that you never expected *my* son to be the Destroyer. You foolishly thought my Eryck was safe. That I would never have a Dreamer child once you took my future away! But I did! And I'm sure you are just furious."

"Jẹ ipalọlọ! Ti o aláìgbọràn ọmọ![4]" That was the anger that Kyia had expected. "I don't know why you can't just be the daughter that I deserve!"

"Do you even hear yourself? The daughter that 'YOU' deserve? You want to be like humans so bad, but you have no idea what it means to be a mother...not a human mother. You can't get past your compulsion to obtain power! I am sure Pherron is no different. How did he become Saran's warrior, Mother? I'm sure he was not linked to her bloodspirit. You have manipulated everyone! But you just didn't plan on Eryck, did you? He will destroy this world...*your* world! He will tear down everything you have built! And the humans will start again...without you!"

---

[4] Be silent! You disobedient child!

Anya stood before Kyia and slapped her hard across the face. "You have tried for centuries to ruin everything that I have created...everything I have created for *you*! You think I know nothing about being a mother. Why do you think I did all of this? For centuries, I have survived to become queen of this world so that you would inherit everything. But you...you are just ungrateful!"

"Please don't act like all of this is for me. O ti wa ni fun o!⁵" Kyia spat out the words.

"Ohhhh! So you do know something of your heritage? I thought you had forgetten it all."

"And whose fault would it be that I had forgotten? You imprisoned me on Drome for how many centuries? You took everything away and now you claim to have done all of this for me. You are such a hypocrite and liar. I have suffered enough, just end this! End me! I don't want to live to see you kill my son. I don't want to live to see you hurt Saran or Yanieyl."

"Kyialles, I would..."

"Stop calling me that! I am not Kyialles anymore..."

"You claim to hate your heritage, but you kept part of your name...didn't you, *Kyia*? You stayed on Benaly. You married a Dreamer. You have clung to this life at every turn! Surely, death is not what you long for?"

Kyia looked at the woman she had known as her mother...the woman who had placed her in an eternal sleep...the woman who had tortured and murdered so many people. She felt sick. She knew that eventually her mother would kill her. Anya had another child now and no use for her. She did the only thing she knew to do. She turned on her mother and walked to the bed. As she did, she whispered, "Fi ọkàn mi. Fi ọkàn mi. Fi ẹmí mi. Fi ti apakan. Ninu ẹjẹ mi, nibẹ da a anfani

---

⁵ It is for you!

lati ri mi ni irugbin ninu mi ala.[6]" Once to the bed, she collasped.

Anya rushed to the bed and cried out, "Ko ọmọ mi! Olusona! Ran mi mú u pada![7]" Men entered the room in the same flash of light that had brought Anya, but she knew that it was too late. Kyia had killed herself.

Yanieyl was sleeping on the blanket. Eryck wanted to look at the tunnel walls more, but he was afraid of what might happen. He watched his beautiful wife sleep and thought of everything they had learned. Was she dreaming now? And if she was, what was she dreaming? As he thought of this, Yanieyl rose up slowly.

"Hey sleepyhead!" Eryck teased, but she did not respond. "Yani, are you ok?"

"Eryck, my son. I don't have much time."

"Yani?"

"No, my love. It's me, your mom. I am channeling your powerful baby inside Yanieyl. Eryck, there are so many things I couldn't tell you. There are things that I was not fully truthful about because they would be hard for you to understand...hard for any human to fathom. But, I wanted to warn you before it's too late. I should be able to come to you through your child always; but I won't be able to come to you like your other ancestors through your dreams...I am not a Dreamer. You must learn your heritage. You cannot trust Anya or Pherron. Anya has an agenda. Everett is her guardian, but he has always held high allegiance to humankind. He loved Naomi and her family, and I know he will help you; but you must speak to him away from Anya. Do not trust her...do not..." Yanieyl began to shake her head violently.

---

[6] Save my soul. Save my heart. Save my spirit. Save that part. In my blood, there lies a chance to see my seed in my dreams.

[7] Not my child! Guards! Help me bring her back!

"Mom! Mom!" Eryck held Yanieyl's hands in his and tried to speak to his mother. But as he looked at Yanieyl, he knew his mother was gone.

"Mom? Eryck, are you ok? What's going on?" Yanieyl curiously looked from the blanket to Eryck.

He slumped along the wall and the lights went out in the tunnel. "She's gone. She was...she was speaking through you...through the baby. I have to go back to Benaly. I'm going to get you somewhere safe and then I need to go back."

"I'm not leaving your side, Eryck Brown. I don't even know why you think I would."

"Yani, if it's not safe in Benaly, you need to be somewhere you can have the baby safely, away from all this craziness."

"If it's not safe, I need to be with you!"

Eryck could see that there was no point in arguing with Yanieyl. He wished he knew how far he was from the house or the exit to the tunnel. As he pondered this, a light flickered in the now dark tunnel. It started small at the corner of the wall and grew until the silhouette of a person appeared.

Eryck grabbed the bag he brought and pulled out a knife. He stood in front of Yanieyl and whispered, "When I say go, I want you to run as fast as you can." Yanieyl nodded and held onto the back of his shirt.

"Eryck, it's Papi. Don't be afraid. Naomi sent me here."

With relief, Eryck put the knife down.

Back at the cottage, Eryck was able to rest with Yanieyl in Saran's loft. It was weird to be back there again, though they had just left the day before. Everything was different now. Everything looked different. Now, they knew about a new world. A world where Saran was alive and not dead. A world of hope...a world of fear.

Papi had talked to him the night before. Naomi put Papi through a series of Dreamer procedures so that he could channel her Dreamer bloodline, memories, and in some instances her powers. They had left Benaly after Saran's disappearance to prepare for a time that Naomi would be gone. He had gone through several blood transfusions to ensure that he could properly channel her and use her dream powers. He was able to locate Eryck that way and retrieve him from the tunnels. Naomi had come to his dreams to tell him how.

"Ercyk, Nana told me to come for you. She said that you can't hide from your dreams, son. We have to face this. We will do it together. We'll get back to the cottage and talk everything out." Papi had told him this while they were still in the tunnels.

But Papi didn't seem know about Kyia, and Eryck didn't tell him. Eryck wasn't ready to trust anyone.

Eryck wanted to find out as much as he could before he revealed what he knew. Yanieyl slept peacefully in Saran's bed and Eryck thought about what it would be like when Saran returned. It had been several years for them, but how much time had it been for Saran? Would she return with Pherron? What would she say to them? Yanieyl started to toss and turn. Eryck couldn't help but wonder what her dreams held. The last time she had slept, he had spoken to his mother. Would Kyia come to him again? As he thought this, Yanieyl opened her eyes.

"Hey bae!" Yanieyl said as she smiled at Eryck, but he just sighed. "Well, don't look so sad." Yanieyl countered his heavy sigh.

"No, I'm sorry...I was just thinking that the last time you slept my mom came to me. When you opened your eyes, I just thought it was her again." He kissed her gently on the forehead. "How'd you sleep?"

"It was good. I didn't dream of anything that I remember and I feel great. Where's Papi?

"He's downstairs making us breakfast. It smells like Nana."

Yanieyl sniffed the air and smiled. It smelled like old times.

Before they could get downstairs, the doorbell rang. The nervousness from the previous day's events startled them and they readied themselves to run. They heard Papi open the door and speak to the visitor.

"I'm glad you came. I know you don't have much time. They're upstairs. I'll call for them."

Papi called up to Eryck and Yanieyl, "Guys, you up?"

"Yes, Papi!" Yanieyl replied. She looked apprehensively at Eryck. She moved closer to him and whispered, "Who do you think it is?"

"I don't know. I'm going to look first." Eryck quietly moved to the ledge of the loft and peered over the side. He couldn't see who was standing there, but he was sure there was more than one person.

"Guys, come on down. There's someone here that you should talk to."

As Yanieyl began walking down the steps, Eryck heard a voice that sounded familiar: the voice from the woman at the Massive Tree - the one called Anya.

They walked down the stairs of the loft to see twelve men, all 6'3" or taller, standing in a semi-circle around a woman just as tall as they were. Each man had a bald head but a variety of skin tones for every color of humankind: Dark brown skin to pale white skin. They stood shoulder to shoulder with their arms crossed at their chests. Each held an intense face of seriousness. None of them wore shirts, but each had on black pants that looked as if they were made for soldiers. They all adorned dark purple capes around their shoulders that were linked together by a cloud shaped clip. Each clip had what appeared to be three lightning bolts through it.

The woman, who looked to be six feet tall without heels, stood regally with her head held high. She had long, thick black hair with streaks of gray and white highlighting it. It was woven into a thick braid down her back and around her forehead was a headband with a diamond in the shape of a cloud with a gold, crescent shaped moon in the middle. To the right of the moon symbol were four sapphire stones that resembled small stars. Eryck instantly recognized the moon and stars as that of the brand inside Saran's wrist.

Eryck and Yanieyl slowed as they approached the group. Eryck felt uneasiness develop in his stomach. He instantly remembered his mother's words about this woman: 'Do not trust her'. He reached for Yanieyl's hand and she responded in kind with a squeeze.

"Hello, Eryck Brown and Yanieyl Starwell. I am Anya Gullivan. How are you?"

Eryck spoke first, "We're good. Nice to meet you. We're just about to eat and head to the Massive Tree to prepare for Naomi's funeral. Did you know her?" Eryck wanted to test out Anya to see what she would say or do.

"I did not know Naomi Moorlander well. I believe she was close in age with my...with Everett Gullivan. I came because Roderick had some concerns about you."

While looking at Papi apprehensively, Eryck quickly responded, "I think we're fine. Thanks for your concern."

"But Eryck," Papi began, "this woman can help you. She knows way more than I do."

"We talked, Papi. We're good and rested now. After the funeral, we're going to head back home to New Charleston. We really left the whole Benaly thing behind us when Saran died and I just want to get back to my own bed." Yanieyl joined in while rubbing her protruding belly. She had learned to deflect attention from unwanted topics throughout the many years when the three friends would investigate the Brown family on their own.

"Eryck," Anya spoke directly to Eryck, barely acknowledging Yanieyl, "you come from a long line of powerful people. I am sure you have several questions or concerns for me."

"Actually, I don't. I understand that my family can interpret dreams, and I guess it's cool and all; but I really just want to start *my* family. We've suffered a lot of traumatic losses over the past few years. I'm going to stay for Nana's funeral, see my mom, and then get on the road." Eryck tried to sound nonchalant when he mentioned his mother, though he felt immense heartache at the idea that he may never see her again.

Anya looked agitated as she attempted to speak to Eryck again, "I...I really don't think you understand the gravity of your role in all of this."

"My role? In Naomi's funeral? Papi, did you have something specific you want me to do? I can speak on behalf of Saran if you'd like." Eryck continued to maintain his clueless demeanor.

"No, Eryck, I don't think that's what she means." Just as he spoke these words, Papi registered that Eryck and Yanieyl's reluctance was on purpose. He looked from Eryck to Yanieyl, then back to Anya. He coughed and said, "Well, Anya, it looks as though I've made a mistake. These young people are doing just fine. I guess it was grief that brought them here. Will you be in attendance at the funeral?"

He began moving towards Anya and the twelve warriors that accompanied her. He could see that this was not what she intended, but Naomi had always told him that everything in their world was not as plain and simple as one would think. Since he was still learning about the dream world, he decided to follow his nephew's lead instead.

"So be it, young Eryck. If you have *any* questions, please contact me. Roderick knows how to reach me." With clear indignation, Anya turned to leave. One warrior opened the door for her, while six warriors led the way. She followed the first six, while the remaining six followed behind her.

Before getting in her stretch limousine, she stopped for one last word, "Eryck, there are many things that you don't know. I believe you will need me and my warriors soon. Come to me when you do." Eryck understood her clearly. It wasn't a request; it was an order.

Everett Gullivan waited patiently as Anya's entourage pulled up to Gullivan Manor. He stood at the top of the stairs where he had stood when she left decades previously. He loved his sister, but he feared her ambition. He remembered the purpose for Dromite Warriors inhabiting this realm at the beginning of time. He remembered their love for Dreamers before it was diluted with human beliefs and activities. He remembered who she was supposed to be as the Queen of Drome.

"Where is Eryck?" Everett asked as Anya approached the steps leading into the manor. Everett's opaque eyes hid his emotions and the indignation that he felt towards Anya.

"That idiot! He wouldn't even talk to me. He didn't even acknowledge that his mother was gone. And I'm not sure he even shared that information with Roderick. What *did* that imbecile say when he called you?" Anya's anger was emanating from her like steam from a pot of boiling water.

"I told you that I should have been the one to go." Everett spoke in a matter-of-fact tone, but there was a subtle hint of superiority behind his words. "He said that Eryck and Yanieyl had come to the house late last night and that they had experienced some strange things. He was very vague and said that he didn't know what to do or tell them."

Everett had found it strange that Roderick had called in the first place, but he also knew that Naomi still had a little faith in Everett even though she had lost much of her belief in the elders of Drome as well as her belief in her own family. Surely, she would have spread this distrust to her husband.

"What do you hope to gain from bringing Eryck here, Anya?" Everett still did not understand the plans or goals of his younger sister.

"He is supposed to bring hell to Earth...Possibly destroy our own home on Drome! I want to contain him! Prevent doom from coming to Earth! Isn't that our purpose?" Anya continued to talk as she stormed passed Everett into the house. "*You* are supposed to be my advisor!"

"No, I am supposed to be your guardian. My role is to guide you in the right direction. That is hard to do when you don't listen to me. At any rate, I cannot advise you on matters I am unaware of. Apparently, I'm not a good guardian or advisor!"

Anya let out an exacerbated sign, "You always say that, Everett. You can guide *and* advise me; you are my big brother first before all else. *We* need to figure out how to get Eryck here. We lost Kyialles which means we lost leverage over the boy. I still think we need to bring Saran and Pherron back. Pherron should be here and I should be back on Drome. I hate Earth!"

"As I have said before, I don't think that Saran should return. If anything, let Pherron return and allow Saran to train with a different warrior."

"No! It is imperative that Pherron be the one to train her!"

"As I said, I cannot advise you on matters of which I am unaware." Everett was done with the conversation. He began to walk away, "I am going to prepare to say goodbye to an old friend, Anya. Be wary of the Dreamers and Warriors who will return to pay homage to Naomi. We will need to monitor the gates to Drome closely now."

Everett turned to walk away knowing that his indifference had angered Anya further. He wanted to know her plans, but he couldn't push. He heard her breathe another heavy sigh as he walked through the outer door to the kitchen.

Left alone, Anya sat in a large chair. No warriors. No servants. No Everett. Alone, she could think about her ultimate plans. Her plan to rid the world of humans. Her plan to dominate the world with a master race of Dreamers and Dromites. Eryck was the key to this. Unlike Principal Dreamers and their blood-sworn Warriors, Eryck was the product of a Dormant Dreamer. Dormant Dreamers rarely were involved in the dream world. Many had grown to think their Principal Dreamer family members to be crazy as humans began to lose touch with their dreams. He was the first of his kind; and according to prophecy, he was supposed to be the last. She would make sure that this did not happen.

"Holt, come to me!" Anya called for her trusted Warrior. He was the first warrior she had taken from his blood-sworn Dreamer.

"Your majesty!" Holt was the largest of the twelve royal warriors. He had pale white skin with thick, wooly, and blond hair. His eyes were gray with what looked like specks of pick crystals.

"I want Eryck Brown brought to me before the ceremony of Naomi Moorlander. He needs to be trained to serve me! Get him. Put him in a sleep-state. Erase the memories of his wife and his wife's memories of him. He needs no distractions. It's time that he meets his true grandmother!" A goblet of wine materialized in Anya's hands. She sipped it with contentment. She *would* have her way.

Holt replied with his hand over his heart and his head bowed, "As you have commanded, so will it be!"

THE BIRTH OF A MASTER WARRIOR

Yanieyl took a long shower. Though she had rested well in Saran's bed, she was still fatigued. She could feel the baby move more and she felt hungry all of the time. Her shower-time was when she relaxed the most. She took this time to think about everything that she had married into. She thought about the potential of having her best friend back. She felt excited and nervous at the same time. Eryck was right. They didn't know what it would be like to have Saran back, and that scared her.

As she was finishing up, she heard a light tap at the door. "Yani, can I come in?"

"Yeah, I'm almost done." Yanieyl hated to admit it, but she was self-conscious of her growing body. She had always been a "thick" girl, but having a huge belly was different-even if it was because she was having a baby. Her breast hurt and she was getting stretch marks on her legs. Her hair was long and thick but barely manageable. She definitely didn't want Eryck to stare at her like that. She cut off the water and grabbed the towel while the shower curtain was still closed.

"You *do* know that I am your husband and I've seen you naked like a thousand billion times, right?" Eryck chuckled as he stated the obvious.

"Yes, I do know you have seen me naked like a thousand billion times. But you haven't seen me naked *and* pregnant!" Yanieyl couldn't help but to laugh at their banter. This felt normal. This felt like their normal life; the life she missed. She felt instant guilt realizing that she missed the life she had without Saran in it.

Eryck interrupter her thoughts again, "So, I'm gonna run a quick errand and come back to get you before the funeral. Is that ok?"

"Sure, once I finish getting dressed, I'm heading over to my folks' place. I haven't seen them since we came back and I'm sure they're wondering why I haven't been by. Do we have a plan for after the funeral? I know you wanted Anya to believe we're leaving, but I know better than that."

Eryck eyed his intelligent wife, "I guess you do know me pretty well. Yes, I have a plan. After the funeral, we are going to act like we're leaving, but we're really going back into those tunnels. This time we're taking more supplies. I want to check out that wall from beginning to end and I want to see where the tunnel lets out."

"Ok, that'll work. I'll see you in a little while." Yanieyl kissed Eryck goodbye and began getting dressed for yet another Brown funeral.

Eryck felt bad lying to Yanieyl, but he wanted to speak with Everett Gullivan before the funeral; and he needed to do it alone. He headed to Gullivan Manor. Part of him felt that going there would be dangerous, but the other part of him felt drawn to the manor. He couldn't explain it; but since he had spoken to his mother, he had been overly conscious of the mark on his neck. He had gone years without really thinking about it; but since she had told him about their past, he had been thinking more and more about it. Seeing the symbol on the walls of the tunnel and on the clips worn by the warriors only made him more curious.

When he arrived at the manor, he felt warmth coming from the brand on the back of his neck. He reached for it only to feel that it was cool to the touch. Immediately he was apprehensive about going into the manor, but he pressed forward motivated by the possibility of learning the truth about his family as well as providing safety to his wife and child.

As he got out of the car, he noticed that the manor door was opening and the 12 warriors that had accompanied Anya were walking out. In the middle of the procession was Anya, tall and regal as ever.

"Why, Eryck? What a pleasure to see you? How may I help you today?" Anya sounded especially sweet which Eryck took to be a charade. Her voice reminded him of the grandmother in *Hansel and Gretel* preparing to eat the children.

"I've come to see Everett Gullivan. I know he is alive and he is here." Eryck tried to sound strong; but in reality, he was nervous.

"Everett isn't available. Is there anything *I* can help you with?" Anya looked way too eager which further alarmed Eryck.

"No, thank you. Papi mentioned that Everett and Naomi were sort of friends and I wanted to see if he would be attending the funeral. I know many people around here thought he had died in the fire...some folks like to keep their privacy."

"So, you came *all* the way over here to ask him that?" She didn't sound convinced, so Eryck continued.

"Well, I don't know a phone number over here and I was out running errands. It was easier to come to the house than find someone with a phone number for a dead man, you know?"

Eryck gave a half-hearted chuckle at his own remark. He looked at Anya and realized that the closer she came to him, the more his neck began to burn. Was the brand on his neck a signal for danger? Slowly, Anya moved away from her warriors. Instantly, Eryck noticed one lone warrior eyeing him stalwartly.

Between her slow movement and his long gaze, Eryck began to feel defensive. His initial instinct was to plan out how he could get away from twelve large men who seemed pre-prepared for any number of possible attacks. He then realized that he had clinched his hands and hoped that no one had noticed. He was wrong.

"Eryck, you look...nervous," Anya purred through a false smile while still moving in his direction.

"To be honest, you and your men don't make me *feel* very comfortable." Eryck decided to go with the truth. The honesty of his words gave him strength and he realized that it was the best thing he had done all day...tell the truth.

"As a matter of fact," he continued, "I feel like you want something from me. Since you keep asking me, how about I ask you: Is there something I can help *you* with?" Eryck automatically moved into a protective stance.

"Hmmm, well, yes, Eryck Brown...yes, you can." Anya looked to the lone warrior who suddenly looked larger than the rest of the men. "Holt, could you show Eryck what I need help with?"

The larger warrior instantly jumped towards Eryck to grab him. Faster than Eryck could have imagined, he dodged the warrior and leapt into the air. As he rose higher, he looked down to realize that he had jumped over the warrior called Holt and landed behind him. The other warriors crouched while waiting for orders from Anya. She stood wide-eyed and then motioned for them to help Holt.

The remaining warriors came towards Eryck while Holt turned in disbelief. Eryck quickly side-stepped four of the warriors in enough time to hit an unsuspecting warrior coming behind him directly in the chin. Immediately he continued his defensive attack by hitting two other warriors and kicking another. As he fought his way through eleven warriors, he was conscious of the larger warrior he had leapt over. Where had he gone? As soon as he thought of him, Holt emerged ready to grab Eryck again. This time Eryck slid between the warrior's legs and ran towards the school leaving his car in the driveway of the manor. The adrenaline in his system prevented him from looking back; he simply ran with no real destination in mind.

As he slowed, he looked to see that he had run straight passed the school and headed for the Massive Tree. At the tree was a single figure...Everett Gullivan.

The man at the tree never turned around, but he spoke solemnly, "I'm sorry for what my sister is putting you through." Eryck barely had time to catch his breath. He looked inquisitively towards the man who had not bothered to look back but apparently knew that he was there. Everett turned around to face Eryck.

"She thinks that she knows what is best. We do need to talk to you. We do need you. But her methods...her methods are less inviting. For some reason, she doesn't see that. She thinks everything must be done by force."

He continued to move closer to Eryck which prompted Eryck to go on high alert. "Eryck Brown, I do not follow my sister's beliefs...or her methods."

Eryck looked at the older man standing before him and started at the elder's white eyes. He tried to imagine how Everett could be a sibling to Anya. Anya looked to be the same age as his own mother, and Everett looked older than even Nana or Papi. He stood with a hump in his back and he moved slowly as if everything hurt in his joints and limbs. In fact, Everett looked like he was Anya's grandfather or great-grandfather even...far from her brother.

"Eryck, you need not fear me. I have no warriors, nor do I have a desire to capture or hurt you. In fact, Anya doesn't want to hurt you...though I fear she does want to capture you. I believe that you would willingly come with us if you truly understood the future turn of events. Would you be willing to listen to an old man?"

Eryck looked at the man. He hadn't said one word since he had run up to the tree, and he still didn't know what to say. He had just gone to speak with this very man just a moment ago, but the attack had changed everything. He felt as if he couldn't trust anyone. In the back of his mind, he heard his mother's voice: *You must speak to him away from Anya.*

"My mother...she said that I could talk to you." Eryck finally spoke and his voice sounded strange to him. He had not had a moment to process the events that had just happened. He had just fought eleven huge men. He had jumped higher than he had ever jumped in his entire life! And now, he was standing with a man that had supposedly died decades ago.

"Anya will be coming here soon. I suggest that we venture to Naomi's cottage to speak. I can place a protective ward on the home that will temporarily conceal us while we discuss the events that have occurred. I can also tell you about your mother and your cousin, Saran."

With that revelation, Eryck was convinced. He would go with Everett and find out as much as he could. From there, he and Yanieyl could create a real plan and they could get his mom and Saran back for good.

Papi heard the knocks on the door but hesitated to open it. He hadn't had time to grieve for his wife before her family's world had come down on him. When they were married, Naomi had told him that her family had secrets...deep dark secrets. She had wanted to stay away from Benaly and the secrets it held. As children, he never noticed this. They were just summer playmates on Benaly and he'd had no reason to pry into her life then. But once they ended up at the same college, he was intrigued by the elusiveness of his girlfriend. He found her mystique to be enticing and magical; she would share small secrets about her dreams and how she could predict certain events through her dreams.

Naomi would walk outside, sniff the air, then declare that rain was coming. Sure enough, it would rain within the hour...sometimes sooner. She would dream of fish then declare that someone she knew was having a baby; within days, she would get a call with news of pregnancy. After they married, Naomi knew well before their daughter told them that she was pregnant with Saran, having told him months before Allayna called with the news. And after many years, he became accustomed to her superstitions and psychic ways; soon forgetting that she held mysterious secrets about her past that he didn't know.

So, when Saran displayed "magical" powers during her senior year, it was both a shock and a relief at the same time. The horror of seeing her harm Naomi was both terrifying and confirming. It also gave Naomi the chance to fully tell her story and share with him the burden she had carried for so long. After Saran left with Pherron, Naomi and Roderick had gone back to their home near New Charleston and Naomi had taught him everything she could about being a Dreamer.

He underwent blood transfusions and was put into deep sleeping comas with the hopes of being able to do half of what Naomi could do with her Dreamer capabilities. She explained to him that Dreamers were humans that had developed special powers by connecting to their own ancestors, internal spirits, and personal energies. They had begun to doubt that he could have Dreamer powers until after the third transfusion when he realized he could actually remember each and every dream he had at night; something he had never been able to do before. He could even see into the dreams of Naomi and talk to her in them. She began to teach him healing meditations and chants, incantations that provided peace to the restless, and chants that would create portals to different places on Earth.

Towards the end of her days, she finally explained where Saran had gone and what she would be responsible for. He knew there was more to it, but she went to sleep a few days ago and never woke up. Naomi knew that the transfusions would take years from her life, but she also knew that Roderick would never understand her world without them; so, she sacrificed her life for her only love so that he could truly understand her and their family.

Papi thought of her now. He thought of what she had given up so that he could just understand his wife, his daughter, and his granddaughter. And he doubted whether it was worth it. Was knowing about this world worth the love of his life?

As he reflected, he moved towards the incessant knocking at his door. There was no going back. He was part of this world now, whether he wanted to be or not. He opened the door to see his nephew and the man that he felt started all of the drama from the last few tumultuous years of his life: Everett Gullivan. With indignation towards Everett, he allowed the two men into the cottage. As Naomi had told him on many occasions: In the Dreamer world, the drama never ends.

"Good morning, Roderick."

"Hello...Eryck, I didn't hear you leave this morning. Yanieyl just left a little while ago. Everett, what brings you by with my nephew this morning?" Roderick didn't dislike Everett, but he didn't exactly like him either. Naomi and Everett shared a past that Roderick was just coming to understand, and he was both envious of Everett and angry with him for bringing his family back into the Dreamer life.

"Anya made her move against Eryck."

With those words, Roderick was no longer angry. He was just concerned about the future of his family.

"Come on and have a seat. I guess there is a lot to discuss." He motioned for Everett and Eryck to sit down.

"Not yet, my friend. We need to protect the cottage. I don't want Anya to know that we are here. She will come here next to find Eryck...especially after he has displayed such strength and defeated her warriors."

Eryck looked at Papi as the shock registered across his face. Eryck was equally shocked because he had yet to tell Everett anything about what happened at the manor, but the old man seemed to know already.

Everett began to chant slowly as he walked to each corner of the cottage: "*Bò o ile pelu ojiji ati òkunkun. Pa o ailewu koja li oju awon ti o fe lati te.*[8]"

He repeated this over and over until both Eryck and Roderick felt like a blanket lay around them. Though Papi had seen so much over time and Eryck was beginning to see so many strange turns-of-events, they were both amazed at what was happening before their very eyes. Everything about the day was simultaneously surprising and scary.

"Will...will that keep her out?" Eryck stuttered.

"No, Eryck, it won't keep her out...but it should temporarily keep her from looking in the house. It will appear that the cottage is vacant. She will not hear our voices or see anything if she looks into the windows. Which she would consider above her anyway...she would make her warriors look. They definitely would not be able to see or hear us. We can speak freely now."

Eryck immediately started, "What the heck's happening in my life?!? Just 30 minutes ago, I fought off eleven men! I jumped over a man I know had to be 6' 5"...maybe taller. I moved faster than even I can imagine. I'm so glad Yani wasn't there; she would have freaked! Every time I wake up in this

---

[8] Cover thee house with shadow and darkness. Keep thee safe beyond the sight of those that wish to enter.

freaking town, there is something else crazy happening. Dreams...magic...ancient people. Hell, my own mom! Which, by the way, I want to know where she is and that needs to be the first thing you tell me!"

"Ok, son, just calm down. I will tell you everything I know. And as you see, I know quite a bit. I cannot promise that I will have time to tell you everything you want to know in the time we have, but I promise I will tell you everything you need to know."

Everett began by telling Eryck what happened to his mother. He told her that Kyia was actually the daughter of Anya and that Anya had done terrible things to Kyia. He wouldn't elaborate because he felt there were more important things that Eryck should know, but he took the time to tell Eryck that she had taken her own life believing that it was the only way to keep him and Yanieyl safe. Everett knew more than anything that Kyialles would want her son to know her fate and to have peace. Everett made sure to tell him that he would always have a connection to her as long as his blood continued to flow through his children.

Eryck cried as Everett told him the news he had already felt a day before, but he listened intently.

He continued by explaining that Saran was safe and sound with Pherron being trained to use her True Dreamer powers. And he ended with the legend...the prophecy of Saran and Eryck.

Everett looked at Eryck and said the words that were told to him millennia before:

> There will come a time when
> humans will become self-
> absorbed. They will eat foods
> that are harmful to their
> bodies. They will wage war on

*each other. They will be
tricksters amongst their own
people. They will become
involved in drugs and fluids
that alter their minds and
prevent them from dreaming.*

As Eryck listened, he realized that so much of the prophecy had already occurred. Everett continued by telling him that "dreaming" was an important part of Earth's life cycle. Dreams were portals to the souls of humans. They allowed people to have compassion for others. They allowed people to have positive desires and ambitions. All of which were healthy for their minds and bodies. But by losing touch with their dreams, humans became liars and thieves. They no longer had positive desires. They no longer had good dreams, which meant the world became living nightmares.

The unknown Creator of Earth had connected all lives together; some called it the Circle of Life. Through selfish ways, religions had distorted the Creator's intentions. The Circle of Life was not just about the food chain of animals; it wasn't just a song on a Disney cartoon. It was truly what kept the Earth spinning on its axis. When the Creator made Earth, it was intended to be inhabited by what the Creator considered its greatest living creation: humans. So, the land, water, fire, and spirit of Earth was connected and fused to one human bloodline: the Brown bloodline. They would be the Dreamers of Earth. They would be the humans that connected the Creator's universe. They would be the humans that controlled the fate of the living plants and animals, the waters and the lands, the spirits and the other humans.

For hundreds of thousands of years, Dreamers lived and reproduced. They found that when they had offspring, only one or two would have the power to connect to dreams and intervene with other humans. Those offspring were declared to be Principal Dreamers and those without powers were considered to be Dormant. Dormant offspring migrated around Earth and reproduced new families, new bloodlines. After time, they were considered to be inferior to Principal Dreamers, but envied all the same.

Principal Dreamers had their lives planned for them. They were united with Dromite Warriors that helped them understand their powers and their purpose on Earth. Principal Dreamers began to feel burdened by their responsibilities and longed to leave Benaly and the constraints of the Dreamer life.

Like the Brown bloodline, the Gullivans were the only Dromites that were permitted to come to Earth with the sole purpose of guiding the Browns. The Gullivans were a sacred family on Drome, one of the original families; and they consisted of a small number of warriors who traveled throughout time between Drome and the Creator's other worlds. While on the dimensional plane of Drome, Time, which was a concept unique to Earth, ceased to exist, which allowed Gullivan warriors to come to Earth and inhabit the planet several times within several millennia. Anya and Everett did not journey to Earth until they had lived for the equivalent of 2000 Earth years on Drome.

Early in their lives, an ambitious Anya became influential with the royal family of Drome and she convinced the then-king to allow warriors from other families to come to Earth. This was not the Creator's intention. Because of this, more and more Dreamers began to be born to families that were not of the Brown bloodline, and more and more Dromite families began to want to inhabit Earth. The Creator did not like this and sent a prophet to Everett with a warning...a prophecy.

> *The prophet foretold the end of Earth and humankind, with one small loophole...the True Dreamer:*
> ### If lies and deceit continue strong,

Then destruction will dry the land.
A Destroyer among thee will overcome,
And thus the end of man.

If Truth shall come to those who believe,
And the family rules the tide,
A True Dreamer will rise above them all
And save the human side.

Because of her fear, Anya had the prophet executed before they could ever understand the prophecy. That was when Everett forged a secret alliance with the Browns of Benaly. He developed an Elder Counsel that created rules for the two families. He'd hoped to stop Dromite Warriors from coming to Earth and prevent additional Dreamer bloodlines from developing. Unfortunately, not only did Anya disapprove of the counsel and its rules, but many of the Brown Dreamers agreed with her.

After several centuries, the families began to fight about the true purpose of Dreamers and Dromite Warriors. Anya, herself, pregnant with a child began to challenge the Elders while petitioning the Dromite king to be his successor. When her child was born, she convinced the king that her daughter was the true heir to the throne and that one of *his* sons had come to Earth disguised as a Dreamer. Because so many Dromites had been finding ways to sneak to Earth, he believed Anya. He granted her succession out of shame of what he believed his son to have done.

Once in power, Anya used her powers to find Seers to interpret the prophecy and she learned that a True Dreamer would be born from the Brown bloodline but a Destroyer would also be born. The Destroyer would be born of a Dormant Dreamer and a shunned Warrior; she just never thought the shunned Warrior would be her own daughter.

After countless years of fighting with her own family, Anya retreated to Drome with her daughter. She ascended to the throne and remained in Drome to find a way to counter the prophecy.

After listening for what seemed like hours, Eryck stood up and turned to face Everett. "That was a lot." Eryck didn't know what else to say. "So, why am I supposed to be the Destroyer?"

"Anya placed Kyialles in a dream state because Kyialles refused to train her Dreamer. She didn't want her life to be chosen by other people. Like so many others of her time, she wanted to fall in love. She wanted to explore the world. She tried to run and hide from Anya, so Anya took her and placed her in a dream-state. At the time, no one had ever actually tried to run away from their responsibilities. They may have grumbled and complained, but eventually they all acquiesced. Kyialles was the first of the Gullivans. I think it was because Anya herself had mated with someone who was not *her* Dreamer that Kyialles was so stubborn."

Everett looked to be in deep thought as he stated this. To hear him speak of his mother with such a strange name made Eryck uneasy. But he continued to listen to the story...to the prophecy.

"By placing Kyialles in the dream-state, Anya 'shunned' her. A Warrior is 'shunned' when they are prevented from connecting with their intended Dreamer. Kyialles stayed in that dream-state for hundreds of Earth years before I released her. Anya still does not know that I am the one responsible for waking her. At the time, I did not know the damage I was doing. I did not know that she was *the* shunned Warrior of legend. After I woke Kyialles, there was a major blowout between the Browns and the Gullivans, Anya forced us all to leave Earth. We faked the fire and our deaths and vowed to never return. I'd hid Kyialles with a family so that Anya would not find her. We had no clue that it was always bigger than us.

"Kyialles met your father, EJ, and fell madly in love. We could observe from Drome, but none of us saw the harm in it. Anya didn't even know that Kyialles was awake and on Earth. The Elders thought that EJ was a 'Principal' Dreamer. We thought it was safe. EJ hid the fact that he was 'Dormant' for many years; so did his mother and siblings. He'd learned the many things that Dreamers foretold and he began to feign Dreamer abilities. He even began to learn how to manipulate his energies."

Eryck looked at Everett. He looked at Papi. Then he sat down with his head in his hands. He felt the weight of everything Everett had shared. He felt a cool breeze on the back of his neck and recognized the truth in the words of Everett Gullivan. He saw the sincerity in his solid white eyes and knew that there were terrible things that would come if he didn't think through his actions. He didn't want to be a Destroyer. He wanted to get his cousin back. He wanted to have a family with the love of his life. He, like so many before him, didn't want his life planned.

With a newfound resolution, he spoke to Everett with wisdom beyond his years, "I don't know what I'm supposed to do. I don't know what the prophecy means. But I know I was not made to destroy. I know that there's more to the prophecy than even you understand, Mr. Gullivan. I can feel it." Everett nodded his head in agreement. "I thought Saran was crazy when she spoke of her strong feelings for Pherron, but now I understand that there's something inside of us that lets us know right from wrong, good from bad, truth from lies. I know..." He looked at Papi, "I know I'm not here to destroy us." Eryck was looking to Papi for reassurance, and Papi returned his gaze with unwavering faith.

Papi nodded to Eryck and then spoke to Everett, "Naomi tried to prepare me for this life. She warned me that it would be hard and there would be liars in our midst. I believe now that you are one of the good guys. You have to help my nephew and my granddaughter. What is it that *you* think Eryck needs to do?"

"Eryck, like Saran, you need to train. And that means you need to leave Earth and travel to Drome. I don't agree with my sister's methods, but I do agree that you need to leave here. There are people coming to challenge everything the Browns and Gullivans stand for. These people will disguise themselves as friends and family, but they will be enemies. I think...No, I know, that you need to go. You will have to leave the life you know and learn to be a Warrior *and* a Dreamer. As soon as the funeral is over, we need to send you to Drome. And you will have to go...alone."

THE DEPARTURE

"Go alone?!? Wait, I can't go alone. I have a wife and child on the way. Saran has been gone for all these years...to 'train.' Surely you don't expect me to leave Yanieyl for that long. She wouldn't understand. I'm not even sure she could survive that after losing Saran."

Everett looked at the young man before him and realized that he was asking for a great deal more than Eryck was prepared to give. But he also knew that if Eryck resisted, Anya would take him by force. He wanted to help the boy. He wanted to help the Brown family. He looked to Roderick for support. "Dear friend, how can this transition be smoother? Anya will continue to come for Eryck. And she cares not about his wife or unborn child. She wants what she wants and there will be very little that will stop her."

Papi thought about the circumstances and he thought about what Naomi would say...what she would do. She was like her ancestors: the Browns that *didn't* want to follow fate. She was a Dreamer that supposedly denied her heritage. She'd never taken the time to meet her Warrior; she'd began avoiding Benaly before it could happen. She wouldn't want Eryck to be taken by force; she would want it to be by his own terms.

Papi looked to Eryck and hoped that he was giving him the best advice. "Eryck, unfortunately, your circumstances aren't ideal. You're damned if you do and damned if you don't. But if you at least try to explain to Yani, then you can train without the burden of lies and we can face this prophecy head on. But if you don't go to train, Anya will continue to pursue you and possibly at the expense of Yani or your baby. I can tell you that Saran made the decision to go...she understood and she knew the costs. But she was willing to pay it to be able to be the True Dreamer that she is becoming...to be able to save the world."

"She knew that she would lose this much time? That we would grieve and believe that she's dead?!?" Eryck was in total disbelief. How could Saran do that to them? How could he even consider doing it to Yanieyl now?

"I don't know if she understood how time would work, but yes, she knew that you would believe that she was dead. But she knew it was for a greater good, so she made the sacrifice. In saving the world, she would be saving you...and Yani. Do you think there was anything in this world that would stop her from doing that?" Papi looked at Eryck with the sympathy he felt Naomi would have given him.

Everett chimed in after Papi, "However...I must caution you. I do not think it wise to inform Yanieyl Starwell. With that knowledge in her memories, other Dreamers or Warriors could access it. She would be at the mercy of anyone who wanted to find you. Your baby would be at the mercy of anyone looking for you or even Saran. Many of the Dreamers and Warriors from different bloodlines want to kill you both. They believe that by killing you, they can prevent the prophecy...and some extremists believe that by ending you and Saran, they can end the pure Brown/Gullivan union. Thus, other Warriors and

Dreamers would have power over humankind that couldn't be controlled. Yanieyl and your unborn child would forever live in danger with the knowledge she would possess... that they both would possess."

"Everett, I need to know more. I can't leave them without a true reason. I can't keep it from her. I can feel that it's wrong thing to do. Please help me understand more."

As Everett listened to Eryck's request, the men felt a shudder and Everett turned to face the front door. Eryck seemed aware that a weight had been lifted from his shoulders, but before he could ask anything there was knocking at the door. A woman began to speak through the door, "Everett! I know you are there. Roderick Moorlander, Open This Door At Once!"

All three men knew the voice immediately to be Anya Gullivan. Eryck reached behind his head to feel his brand beginning to burn.

Quickly and quietly, Everett responded to Eryck, "Ok, Eryck, I truly understand. This is what I'll do, I will come to you in your dreams this evening. It may be painful if I have to force you to sleep, so try to take a sedative. You need to be sleep by 10 o'clock tonight. Somewhere safe, where your body is guarded. And remember, do not tell Yanieyl just yet. Let me explain the dangers first, then you may decide."

When Anya entered the cottage, it seemed as if she floated above the ground. She stepped so lithely that the men barely heard her move. Everett held his head high as if he'd done nothing wrong. Eryck glared at Anya with resentful eyes, not ignoring or refusing the stares of her warriors either. Roderick looked slowly from the tension in his nephew to the eyes of hidden betrayal in Everett to the suspicious demeanor of Anya. He took a deep breath and moved towards Anya. He took her hands delicately in his and bowed to her formally.

"Anya..." he looked from Everett to Eryck, "Your Majesty...Everett has been teaching me about your customs.

Some of which Naomi had previously shared. He told me that *you* are the ruler of Drome! I so am honored to have you in my home again. I didn't know this the last time you were here. I promise I would have treated you differently. I'm so new to all this!" Papi rattled on like a star-struck groupie. Eryck recognized this as Papi trying to buy them time to gather themselves.

Anya was not easily distracted, but to be showered with praise did seem to calm her. "Roderick, as heartwarming as your declaration is, I am actually curious as to why *my* brother has cloaked *your* cottage."

Everett bellowed with a voice much louder than Eryck or Papi had heard him use, "You can ask me yourself why *I* cloaked the home!" As quickly as he lifted his voice, he went back to his lowly stature.

Anya gave Everett a piercing glare, "Well, brother...why *have* you cloaked this home?"

"I did it so that I would know when *you* arrived...since I was sure that you would." Everett replied with a gruff.

"And just how were you *so* sure?" Anya looked innocently at Everett.

"That is not your concern, Anya. Just know that I knew you would eventually come here to get what you want."

"Everett, you always claim to know everything. But there are some things you simply don't know. You have no clue why I am here...just as young Eryck and Roderick Moorlander do not know."

Everett was tired of the banter between the two. "Anya, I am and forever will be an Elder. I am your guardian. But at my core, dear sister, I am also a Warrior. I do not have to explain why the cloak was placed. Simply that I am the one who placed it is enough. *We* are going to bury a dear friend and a strong Dreamer of Benaly: Naomi Moorlander. I will not allow you to sully this day with accusations, ambitions, or selfish ways. I will be escorting Roderick, Eryck, Yanieyl and their family to the Massive Tree and ensuring their safety home."

With this, the final word was said. Eryck called Yanieyl to inform her that they would be picking her up and they all left the cottage.

In the limousine sat Eryck holding Yanieyl's hand, Everett, Roderick, and Anya, who had decided to ride with them at the last minute: presumably to show a united front between the clans.

Eryck hadn't told Yanieyl anything about what had happened that day. She looked rested and pleasant; he didn't want to take that away from her as they attended such a somber event. He knew that with the news of Saran's return, Yanieyl would be a mixture of relief and grief. She leaned into him and whispered, "How was your day running errands? And how did *she* end up with us?"

"Eventful," was all he could manage to say. He exchanged a look with Anya, and in that moment, they shared a look of hatred and anger. Eryck thought to himself, *How dare she try to control my life?* Lies had caused so much destruction in their family. Maybe if Saran had told them the truth they could have helped. Maybe they could have found out his role in everything sooner. Maybe his mom would still be alive...if she only had been honest with him. He realized then that honesty changed everything, and he would tell Yanieyl everything. He would make sure that she was safe by talking to her and having a plan: a plan that they both created and could live with.

As they approached the road that led to the Massive Tree, they were met with traffic: cars with purple flags flying from the front of each car on top of each headlight. Each flag bore the symbol that Eryck recognized again as Saran's brand: An outlined crescent moon with four stars.

"Papi, who are all these people? Nana always said people got on her nerves. She barely spoke to the townspeople; it looks like everyone in South Carolina is here!" Yanieyl asked.

"Well, Yani, Nana was an interesting lady. While people got on her nerves most of the time, people gravitated to her. They came to get counseling from her from all over the world. She gave the best advice...and for some she interpreted their dreams." Papi looked away with eyes watered from the fondness of his wife's memories.

"And the purple flags?" It was Eryck that asked the next question.

Anya spoke then, quietly, in a voice of reverence. "They are the symbol of the Brown family and those who hold allegiance to them." She looked down now, and held her hands together. She squeezed them as if holding in a tremor. Everett reached for her and held her hands in his. They shared a look and it was hard to see whose side each person was on. That there was a war brewing was undoubted, but who were the good guys and who were the bad? It seemed as if they all held this question in their minds as they looked around the car at each other... and then ahead to the Massive Tree where Naomi Moorlander would be laid to rest.

At the Tree, there were hand-carved chairs surrounding the tree: thousands of them. Only one aisle opened through the chairs which led to a large hand-carved wooden mound of intricate detail.

Naomi's body lay wrapped in white silk on a section of the mound surrounded by soft fabric like swirls of clouds. It didn't seem to be physically possible for her to be stable atop the mound, but there she lay.

Eryck and Yanieyl had never seen a funeral like this. It was different from anything they had ever seen in Benaly. They weren't in a church. There wasn't a choir singing old hymns. No preacher or groups of deacons waiting to collect money...Yes, even at a funeral. This was tranquil and solemn. It was angelic and heavenly. It was reverent.

As Eryck looked into Yanieyl's eyes, he heard a quiet chanting coming from the people around him: *Bò ọ pẹlu ojiji ati òkunkun. Pa ọ ailewu kọja li oju awon ti o fẹ lati ma kiyesi. Mimọ idagbere ti Naomi Moorelander.*[9] He remembered some of the words as the words that Everett had used when he cloaked the cottage. He then felt the familiar feeling of a light blanket across him. They were cloaking the funeral. He wondered why the funeral would need to be cloaked. He watched as Everett walked slowly through the single aisle with ten other elderly people behind him in deep purple robes: each one with their hoods covering their faces.

Everett moved around to face Roderick and the rest of the Brown family, all of which wore black with purple crescent moons embroidered in their clothing. It seemed that Eryck and Yanieyl were the only ones to not adorn the familiar insignia of the Brown Family. Suddenly, Eryck felt very conscious of his difference from the rest of his family. He was conscious of his disassociation to everyone. And as he thought about it, he realized that as large as his family was, he only knew Nana and Saran. He didn't recognize any of these people. His brand tingled and he felt strong feelings of jealousy and pain as he continued to sit amongst his 'family.'

As he realized this, he also noticed that throughout the ceremony Anya had not taken her eyes off him. She wasn't there for Naomi at all; she was there for him. He needed to protect his family: his real family-Yanieyl and his baby!

Everett began to speak and Eryck listened as he learned even more about his Nana: Naomi Moorlander.

I have been on this Earth for a long time. I have seen many Brown Dreamers be born into this life and many depart. Naomi Brown

---

[9] Cover thee with shadow and darkness. Keep thee safe beyond the sight of those that wish to observe. The sacred farewell of Naomi Moorelander.

was a strong and rebellious spirit. She fought to preserve the heritage of Dreamers, Warriors, and humankind. We have attempted to preserve the Brown-Gullivan bloodlines for many millennia. And in the past few centuries, we have seen many Brown Dreamers abandon their heritage in favor of a different destiny. And ultimately, it is us...the Gullivan Warriors of Drome... who watch your destinies come into fruition every time.

Naomi left Benaly to forge her own path. Many believed that she ran from her heritage. They feel that she abandoned her Dreamer faith. But I alone know that she never hid...she never abandoned her faith. She simply chose another way. She found love outside of our confines and rules. And she still produced the True Dreamer of legend as an heir. She never forgot her heritage and she shared it with the world: making countless humans more conscious of their own dreams and bringing back the power of Dreamers.

Many thought us to be enemies, but in truth, Naomi Brown Moorlander was a dear friend and confidante. I personally believe that Naomi may have single handedly extended the life of humankind by presenting a new way to bring humans back to honesty and truth...the true purpose of the Brown Dreamer and Gullivan Warrior Bond! To the heavens I say: Mu ọ bi a ayaba![10]

All around the Massive Tree there was a resounding voice that demonstrated unison and power:
Mu ọ bi a ayaba!
Eryck noticed Anya in the midst of all the people around them; all yelling in unison. Anya did not repeat the words of respect as the others did, and her eyes reflected small flecks of

---

[10] Take thee as a Queen!

shimmering red glimmering in her pupils. It was as if Eryck could feel the anger eminating from her. Quietly, he said the words to himself: *Mu ọ bi a ayaba!*

Anya...this woman before him was no queen. He would train...he would prepare...he would stop whatever Anya was planning...he would stop *her*!

The ceremony ended with them lighting Naomi's funeral pyre. In the past, her body would have floated atop the ocean. But without the water, they were unable to do that. So Eryck, Papi, and Yanieyl drove to the new oceanfront. With highrises and restaurants lighting up the night sky, they slowly walked down the pier.

Eryck held Yanieyl's hand as they walked behind Papi who held the remains of Naomi Moorlander in a large urn. At the end of the pier, it seemed that all bystanders had disappeared and they were the only people there. As Eryck held Yanieyl in a deep embrace, Roderick Moorlander bid his wife farewell. Eryck quietly said the words he remembered from the ceremony: *Mu ọ bi a ayaba!*

Yanieyl repeated: *Mu ọ bi a ayaba!*

And finally, Papi repeated: *Mu ọ bi a ayaba!*

As the last of the ashes fell from the urn, steam lifted from the ocean. Fog immediately came in from the west of the pier. It was thick and ominous as the three gathered to say their final goodbyes. As they turned to walk down the pier, they noticed figures standing at the end.

"Who do you think that is?" Yanieyl asked Papi and Eryck.

Papi looked further down the pier but it was too dark. "I'm not sure. Probably new locals or tourists. Let's head back."

They agreed and moved towards the car. Eryck felt behind his head and his brand began to become warm...not like it did when Anya was near him. It was a calming warmth. It felt like...like home.

As they walked towards the car, the steam from the ocean continued to grow and spill over onto the pier. It followed the three of them to the car and the fog seemed to get thicker as they walked. As they drove, it continued to increase; and by the time they had returned to the cottage, they had no visibility in front or behind them.

"This is so weird. We rarely have fog like this around here. Especially since the ocean receded." Papi remarked as he looked around. Eryck looked at his watch. It was already 9 o'clock. He needed to talk to Yanieyl and explain everything to her before he went to sleep so that he could make the best decision for them. Just as he was thinking that, he turned to see that the cottage door was opening.

Papi reacted immediately, "Eryck, be prepared to take Yani."

They walked to the cottage cautiously with impaired vision from the fog. Papi yelled out, "Who's there?!?"

"Papi?" They all heard the voice and stopped in their tracks. "Papi, is that you?"

"Sa-Saran!" Papi gasped. A figure darted out the door and into Papi's arms.

"Papi! I've missed you so much!"

As their eyes adjusted, Eryck and Yanieyl looked on with disbelief as their best friend hugged Papi before their very eyes.

"I can't..." Yani began to talk but couldn't form the words.

Eryck finished Yanieyl's words for her, "I can't believe you're really here."

Saran turned to look at the man before her. "Eryck? Is that you?" She tried to move closer to him, but he backed away. She reached for his face, and he reluctantly allowed her to touch him. "You look...different."

"I look older." Eryck said coldly. He realized how angry he had become over the past few days. "Unlike you," he finished.

"I don't understand." Saran said slowly.

Papi looked around at the gathering fog. It had gotten even thicker as they stood outside. It felt as if he could grab it and shape it. Something did not feel right. He turned to the children, "I think we should go inside."

Once inside the cottage, they were faced with the reality of Saran's choice. She stood before them as the seventeen year old she was when she left; everyone else stood looking much older. She sat quietly as they told her everything that had happened since she left and from where they were returning. "She's gone?" was all Saran could say. "I was only gone for a few days."

"You've been gone for years, Saran, not a few days." Eryck grumbled. Yanieyl had not spoken.

"Where's Pherron?" Saran then asked nervously.

"Where's Pherron? Where—is—Pherron?!? Are you serious?!?" Eryck roared. Yanieyl grabbed his hand and quickly spoke for her husband.

"Saran, we have learned a lot in the past few days. But not nearly enough to understnad why you'd leave with Pherron Black? Why you'd let us believe you were dead? Didn't you think about how we would feel?"

Saran stopped looking anxious and turned to her friends. "I did think about you. I thought about everyone. I left a note that I hoped you find. It was the only thing I had time to do. I can't even explain to you what it was like to be on Drome. To learn what I've learned."

Yanieyl stood up and walked into the kitchen. It was 9:45. She grabbed a glass of water before returning to the den where they all sat looking at each other. Eryck kept looking at his watch, and Papi kept looking at Eryck. Eryck hadn't had a chance to tell Yanieyl what would be happening that night.

They spent the next few minutes arguing about Saran's disappearance, Naomi's death, Papi's transfusions, and finally the events that had led to Kyia's death. As soon as Eryck was beginning to explain the next "big" decision that needed to be made, he felt a sharp pain on his brand. He reached for his neck just as darkness blinded him. He felt his body go limp and then he was no longer in the den of the cottage.

What happened?!? Eryck thought to himself

I had to put you to sleep. Eryck heard the voice of Everett Gullivan in his head, but he didn't see him. He tried to look around but there was nothing but darkness surrounding him. *I told you I would come at 10 o'clock.*

Yeah, well, I thought I had time. You also didn't tell me that Saran would be back.

Quick decisions had to be made. Everett sounded agitated. *I must be honest, Eryck Brown. I have done what I swore not to do. I wanted you to choose to train...on your own, but I see your weakness. I could not allow you to tell Yanieyl Starwell everything. To keep everyone safe, I have taken your soul from your body. To them, you have just died. I am praying that Saran has learned enough while on Drome to know to take you to the Massive Tree to take her place. She was revived, but without Pherron. I couldn't tell Anya this, but by leaving Pherron, I am able to place you in slumber instead of Saran. Anya will still be waiting for Pherron to wake while I get you to Drome. I'll have to figure out another way to get Saran back later. Eryck, open your eyes.*

As Eryck opened his eyes, he saw brilliant swirls of colors around him. There were expanses of water everywhere. In the sky, he saw three brightly shining suns spinning around a large crescent moon. The ground was a mixture of blues, greens, and purples. The sky was an interchanging flow of rainbows. The only constant was the water. The rapidly flowing water that seemed to be everywhere. Everything around him screamed life.

"Where am I?!?" Eryck exclaimed and the world around him trembled. An explosion in the distance sounded off and Everett appeared to him.

"Eryck, welcome to the World of Drome. Here, you will learn how to master dreams and how to use them to guide the world."

"I don't understand."

"I took your soul and brought it to Drome through a sleep-state. I brought Saran back so that you can take her place. Once your body is in the traveling container, Anya will have to have my encantation to bring you back. Only I could revive Saran or Pherron. I brought Saran back so that you can move under the radar."

"And if Saran doesn't get me to the Tree?" Eryck asked impatiently.

"You will die, young Eryck."

"I'll die! I'll die?!? You say that like it's nothing. What about Yani? What about our baby?"

"I had to take the chance. I saw what my sister was about to do. I knew that you would only come if you could tell your wife everything, and I knew that would be catastrophic! Anya would have killed Yanieyl and your unborn child."

Eryck felt a quickening of his heart. He reached for his chest in pain. "What is happening?! I feel like my heart is about to explode."

"We are running out of time," Everett stated.

Eryck grabbed his chest and cried out in pain. "Everett, what have you done?!? I'm dying!"

Eryck fell to the ground with Everett kneeling over his body. Everett placed his hands on Eryck's chest and Eryck felt a weight being lifted and energy soaring through his veins. His brand began to pulse and warm. A tingling sensation began to radiate around the brand and slowly Eryck realized that he was no longer lying on the ground; he was floating through the air. Everett kept one hand on Eryck's chest as he guided his body through the air. Eryck tried to move, but he was paralyzed. He had no control over any part of his body. All he could do was look at the beautiful and mysterious sky above him.

In his peripherial, Eryck began to see lush green leaves. They seemed so out of place in this world, so normal. He felt his body gliding to the ground. He then realized where Everett had guided his body. He was at the Massive Tree, but the Tree was different here. Water completely surrounded the Tree. He wondered how Everett had walked to the Tree, if he had walked at all.

Eryck began to breathe again. His chest felt lighter. Everett looked at Eryck with relief, "She did it. She moved you."

"So, now what?" Eryck asked.

Everett looked at him with mischief and excitement. "Now, young Eryck...now, we train..."

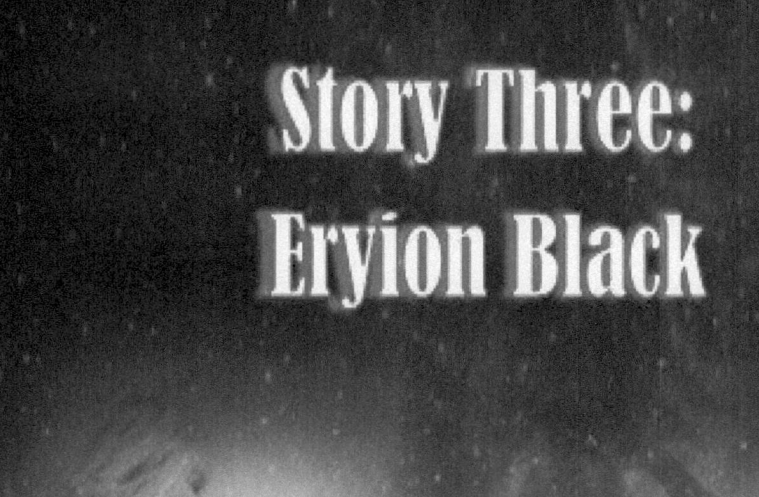

Story Three:
Eryion Black

A True Dreamer's Gain

EARTH...100 YEARS LATER

This is planet Earth. Many decades ago, the oceans, the rivers, and the lakes... they all completely dried out. Some major oceans, like the Pacific Ocean, still had small traces of water on the ocean bed floors; but for the most part, Earth was dry. Many people on Earth attributed the recession of water to Global Warming or an environmental catastrophe caused by the reckless nature of human beings...which wasn't exactly far from the truth. But the truth...the truth was far more complex...the truth was that a super race of humans had failed the Creator. The truth was that Dreamers had lost the war.

Throughout the history of humankind, Dreamers made sure that normal human beings were linked to the rest of the living things on the planet and in the universe. Through humans' dreams, Dreamers were able to encourage normal humans to be kind and honest people. They were able to cultivate their hopes and ambitions. Dreamers were able to show humans the valuable advances that people eventually made in art, music, and technology; they were much like the Greek mythological Muses, who were really Dreamers...except they did so much more than just inspire. They provided balance to Earth. With Dreamers connected to human dreams, all of the Earth remained alive...alive and *protected*.

Several civilizations had been trampled and destroyed by the time The Creator realized that humanity was failing. During the 21st Century of modern man, humans evolved too quickly. They moved beyond just advancing in inventions to make their lives better. They began to advance using man-made chemicals to improve life...to take away life's problems...to wage war...to end life. The same chemicals that were used for so many good, and bad, things in the human world eventually led to humans losing the ability to dream at all.

Without the ability to dream, humans stopped pursuing their hopes or ambitions; they did what was expected of them instead of what they had a passion for...or they did nothing at all. The world had been built by humans' dreams, and then people forgot who had made the dreams happen in the first place. Men and women began to live solely for the sake of money and technological advances. They forgot about art and music, literature and history, agriculture and science. They began to live through computers and technology: caught in a matrix forging fake lives and existences online instead of in the real world. People watched other people's lives, though the other lives were scripted. Everything became false. Everything became untrue. Everything became lies.

Soon, a war began between some of the Dreamers on Earth and their Warriors, a species from the dimensional plane of Drome. Dreamers and Warriors were tasked with keeping Earth alive...keeping humans alive. Once they no longer saw eye to eye on their purpose, Dreamers and Warriors began the end of Earth and humankind...all-natural resources were exhausted, war and disease spread, and the water depleted. Humankind followed suit...slowly dying with the Earth.

For Eryion Black, life was a huge mystery in general; yet he was unknowingly familiar with the world of lies and deceit. He was raised by his Aunt Sa-Ba in a territory called Benaly Centreland. Benaly had been the original home of Dreamers on Earth. At one time, it had been an island surrounded by water, but the Great Water Recession had turned it into a Centreland. A Centreland was an area of land that did not have water near it by creek or river, pond or lake, nor sea or ocean for more than 300 miles.

Centrelands rarely had water in the land for plants to grow, and only a few plants still grew above ground due to the minimal rain that the plants received. Sa-Ba was one of the only people who remembered stories about Benaly as it was before the Great Water Recession.

Most humans had died off during the final years of the water recession. Those that survived had been people who lived mostly as vegans and had taken excellent care of their bodies. The survivors of Earth typically lived underground. Some of the wealthy still lived above ground, but most humans had retreated to structures created for the purpose of living under the Earth's floor. In select areas, scientists had started to learn how to re-create water and had begun attempts to rebuild the Earth as it had been. Sa-Ba was the scientist that taught them all.

On top of being the smartest scientist in the known world, she had taken in Eryion and raised him from near birth. He did not have any memories of life before Sa-Ba; and even more mysteriously, he didn't have memories before the age of six years old either. He found it strange that he didn't remember parents or even childhood friends, but he had become used to the hidden anonymities of his life. Now, he approached his twenty-first birthday, and he felt like he was ready to ask Sa-Ba about the secrets she kept.

Sa-Ba was a different type of "parent." She had always been great to Eryion; but she had strange ways and times when she was extremely distant and cold. Some nights she would sit and talk to Eryion for hours about the old days...days that should have been too long ago for her to remember. Other times, she would go days without saying a word to him or anyone else for that matter. People around the Centreland would describe her as a quirky misanthrope. They knew she was a genius with all of the water and plant technologies she developed, but she didn't have friends. And, occasionally, she could be very rude. In the darkest of corners, she was even described as a witch. Ultimately, she just had Eryion. Eryion became a loner because of this, having only a few associates that he spoke with when he had been school age. He had even fewer now.

As a child, Eryion wanted to know more about Sa-Ba as well as himself. He'd ask around town about Sa-Ba, trying desperately to find out anything about Sa-Ba's life as a child or anything about his real parents; but no one knew her. No one knew anything about the Blacks at all. Supposedly, she just appeared in her cottage fifteen years ago: the summer before Eryion started grade school. She enrolled Eryion in school and then began looking for shelter underground. Even the act of moving underground made Eryion curious.

Sa-Ba insisted that they live underground like majority of the survivors, though she had a very well-built and well-maintained cottage above ground: A cottage that was not devastated by the war or the Great Water Recession. Sa-Ba was different...odd...eclectic. When he got older, he stopped asking her for questions and began looking for answers.

Eryion became a meddler, an inspector of sorts; he liked to pry into things to figure out more about his life, which would occasionally get him in trouble in the community. He knew Sa-

Ba was secretive for a reason, and probably a darn good one; but he still longed to know her secrets as well as the enigmas of his true identity. That meant snooping in areas where he shouldn't be and sometimes in places that were dangerous.

For as long as Eryion could remember, Sa-Ba had kept a journal. She wrote everything down. She had volumes and volumes of these journals, and she kept them in a room that was always locked: whether she was in the room or not, the door was always locked. As a young boy, he would try to sneak into the room and would get caught every time. When he got older, he simply asked her about the room. She answered in a short manner saying it was her 'Library of the Past' and that it held great knowledge and power that *he* would need one day... then she never spoke of it again. When he tried to bring it back up, she would change the topic. That made him even more suspicious about their past, but he knew that continuously asking her was futile.

Still, he didn't have a lot of memories that didn't have Sa-Ba in them. He didn't have any memories of his mother or father, and she never acted like a "real" parent to him. That was one thing that always seemed strange to him. To be with someone your whole life, but still feel like you lived with a stranger. He loved Sa-Ba. He guessed he loved her like he would have a mother, but he always wondered how *she* felt about him.

When Eryion turned sixteen, he asked Sa-Ba about his family...his real parents. She gave only one reply with sadness, "I am your family." She never spoke about it again and he never asked. Eryion spent most of his life keeping to himself always wondering...always wanting.

Today, the day before his twenty-first birthday, Sa-Ba had packed a bag and was preparing to go above ground. He knew that they would be above ground for at least a day or two. This would be the day he got to sleep above ground...look at the stars...and sleep in a large bed. Today was Sa-Ba's holy day.

Very few trees still existed on Earth. However, the tourist attraction that kept Benaly Centreland economically functioning was the Massive Tree. People traveled from all around to see the tree that continued to live without water. Every month, Sa-Ba insisted that they go to that tree and leave offerings to their ancestors. Eryion went each month, but he hated it. He didn't like the way people looked at him above ground. He knew that the Uplanderes, the few people who lived above ground, considered themselves better than the Grounderes.

And, then there was the food...the food above ground was different from the food underground. Ironically, he missed the strange texture of food that had been grown underground in a lab.

But mostly, he hated being near the Tree. When they were near the Massive Tree, Eryion always felt an uncomfortable tingling over his body. He felt like he was being pulled in different directions. The one and only time he had touched the Tree itself, he felt like he couldn't breathe and that his heart was about to stop. He never touched the tree again and he'd hated coming back ever since then; but he never told Sa-Ba and he went every month nonetheless.

As they came above ground in their carriage, they allowed their eyes to adjust to the light. Cars of the past had ceased to exist. Most of the advanced technology that had been created by humans was destroyed in the war. However, small technological advances still remained because of the same scientists that were working to bring back water... the same scientists that Sa-Ba had trained.

There were still machines used for travel; but fewer gas fueled vehicles like airplanes, buses, trains, and traditional cars of the past. Onders, underground vehicles, were much more popular. They were created for underground travel. They removed the need for airport, bus, or train stations; and they removed some of the historic causes of pollution in the air which was believed to contribute to the Global Warming that dried the waters of the world. The Onders were powered from underground soil and were the generation of mobile technology that was created after Sa-Ba's carriage: the Vervoer.

The Vervoer was the first-generation vehicle used for travel above and underground. But they only operated on the ground; they couldn't be used in the air or in water. It required the use of a manual peddle system with support from a soil based energy source but far less soil than what was used for the Onders. Even with the manual effort that was needed, Sa-Ba favored the Vervoer all the same. Sa-Ba said she thought using a manual system would keep them stronger than humans who quickly accepted the fast technology of the Onders...and being strong is how some humans had survived the Great Water Recession and others didn't.

The summer sky held a large sun with no clouds to cover it. Eryion and Sa-Ba immediately put on their sunglasses as they entered the troposphere of Earth. It was sweltering with heat and Eryion realized he had on way too many clothes. Underground, the temperature was typically cool and they wore many layers of clothing. Above ground was drastically different, so he started to shed a few layers.

"Soooo, Sa-Ba, what are you leaving the ancestors today?" Eryion asked whimsically, attempting to sound enthused about their day. He never wanted Sa-Ba to know how much he hated coming to the Massive Tree, no matter how much he *did* love coming above ground.

"Well, I brought some fruit and some vegetables." Sa-Ba looked around like someone else was in the carriage. Then she leaned a little closer to Eryion and said quietly, "I also brought a plant that I been growing for 20 years...give or take."

Sa-Ba always referred to time in estimations: "20 years give or take," "around about 20 years or so," "'round 'bout that time." No time was ever exact with her. And as he thought about this, he realized he didn't even know how old Sa-Ba was. Even with her age, she would tell people that she had been "around the block a time or two" but never a specific age.

"You mean that little potted plant that sits under the special lights in your lab?" Eryion asked and Sa-Ba nodded in confirmation.

Eryion loved visiting Sa-Ba's lab. It was the one place where he felt closest to Sa-Ba...when she shared the most information with him. She was able to help other scientists who traveled to Benaly to learn how to reproduce many of the Earth's natural resources in her lab. It was the place that made her famous.

Part of her lab was underground in their home station, but she had a relatively small garden that was above ground as well. The lab underground was expansive. The walls of the lab were bright white from smoothed quartz, and there was a variety of lighting systems used to grow many different agricultural things underground.

Towards the center of the lab was a clear quartz-enclosed office with a circular escalator that wound around to the surface of Earth. As you rode the escalator 200 feet above the surface, the minerals that were left in Earth's soil shined radiantly. You could also see various plants that had begun to grow in the Earth due to the work that Sa-Ba was doing and teaching to others.

The lab was Eryion's special place to go and think.

Sa-Ba had new vegetables and fruits that had never existed before. She had flowers and herbs. She had a small pond, developed from artificial water, with fish in it that circled her crystal office. It was like an oasis...his and Sa-Ba's personal oasis.

In her office, she grew extraordinarily rare and foreign plants. There was one that always sat separately from everything in a shelter under a one-of-a-kind lighting system; no other plant needed this type of lighting. The leaves of the plant were violet with a crimson ring around it. The veins of each leaf were vibrant red and black. And each leaf was covered with soft white fur. The body of the plant was jet black, not green like most other plants that Eryion had read about in books or seen in Sa-Ba's lab. It was such a strange plant, and he'd always wondered what it was for. But he'd learned that when he just sat back and let Sa-Ba do her thing, he learned more than when he asked tons of questions.

Today was different. Eryion couldn't resist asking about the plant. "Sa-Ba, that funny looking plant...why now?"

"You and your questions! It's time to offer it, is why." Eryion laughed at Sa-Ba. It drove her crazy when he asked a lot of questions, but he knew she had gotten used to it. She tried to sound fussy but even she couldn't fight a huge smile coming across her face. This plant was important. He didn't say anything else about it.

Eryion had been planning this day. Today was Interrogation Day! He would ask Sa-Ba all the questions he'd wanted to know for most of his life. They would have time at the cottage and on the ride back home. Normally, he was exhausted after their trips to the Massive Tree; but this time, he wasn't going to sleep the entire time. He had questions...questions that he would insist that she answer. If she refused, he would give her his ultimatum: He would move away!

He wasn't trying to be mean or spiteful. He didn't *want* to leave her all alone; she was the only family he'd known. But he also didn't want to live another moment of his life feeling trapped...scared to meet new people...avoiding life. He wanted to live.

As he thought about this, he felt his chest begin to tighten and he felt the uncomfortable tingling that had become so familiar start to flow over his body. Today, the feeling was strong and overwhelming. He caught himself gripping the side of the carriage. Sa-Ba noticed this but said nothing. She simply held her lips pursed tight, her smile turning to a well-recognized frown, and she continued to peddle towards the tree...even as Eryion slowed down.

At the Tree, Sa-Ba waited in the Vervoer. Tourists never seemed to bother her in the past. She would jump out of the car with her picnic basket and blanket and then set up around the tree. If people gawked at them, Sa-Ba never noticed or cared. But, today she was apprehensive. She kept looking around her like she had when they were in route to the Tree. She didn't get out immediately; instead, she just sat and watched the people coming and going from the Tree.

Finally, she watched the last tourist walk away from the Tree. They'd sat in the car for over two hours...not saying a word. Sa-Ba didn't try to explain what she was waiting for, and Eryion, for once, didn't ask.

"Ok, E. Let's get a move on. The sun is setting and folks are leaving. We can prepare now."

He was so tense from the tingling that had been going on in his body for two hours that he felt utterly drained when he began to move. He opened the door to get out and began to see small stars circle in front of his eyes.

"Sa-Ba, I feel *real* weak. Did you bring anything to eat?" Eryion turned to look at Sa-Ba, but he was seeing two of her swaying in the driver's seat.

"E, I need you to be strong today. Please fight whatever you are feeling right now." Sa-Ba began to circle her wrist, a habit he had seen her do on many occasions. Slowly, he felt a cool feeling rush over his body like a light breeze. The cool air flowed over his head, around his shoulders, into his blood. He could even smell a breeze...something fresh and salty. "E? Are you gonna to be ok?" Sa-Ba asked.

Eryion reached for the door again to stand up. No more stars. No more tingling. Just a fresh feeling of cool air. He got his bearings and looked around. "I'm good. I'm ready."

He got out of the Vervoer with renewed energy and began to take out the basket and blankets. There was another box in the carriage that he hadn't noticed during the trip above ground. "Do you need this box too?" he asked.

"Yes, you get the box and the basket. I will get the blankets and the plant. We have a long night ahead of us." Sa-Ba headed towards the Tree.

She placed the blankets in front of the Tree in an area that seemed to be worn down. Though the Tree was clearly ancient, with roots protruding from the ground, this area had fewer roots coming out the ground and was actually rather flat-like the Tree had made a natural sitting area.

"Eryion, you will be twenty-one years old in a few hours." Sa-Ba never called him by his full name. She always called him "E"-unless he was in trouble. It had been ages since she had called him that. "I know you've always had questions about your family, your past...me." She looked uncomfortable. "I know you wondered why I wasn't closer to you."

Sa-Ba began to circle her wrist again. The cool breeze became stronger, but Eryion saw no evidence that the breeze was real. Without oceans, lakes, and rivers, breezes weren't something that people felt very often, especially when they were only above ground once a month. Breezes were something you read about in history books. Majority of the Earth was barren like a desert. But sure enough, Eryion could feel a "breeze" now...blowing all around him. However, he also felt the tingling sensation trying to push through the feeling of fresh air.

Sa-Ba took out a small pot and poured a light pink liquid into it. She broke three leaves from the odd plant and placed them into a mortar using a pestle to grind the leaves. She poured the contents into the small pot and placed it over the small fire she'd had Eryion build. After the contents came to a boil, she poured it into two cups. She took one and then offered him the other. For some inexplicable reason, he watched her with caution. When she took a sip of the drink, he took one. They repeated this until the drink was gone for both of them. She began talking again as she circled her wrist and Eryion felt the cool breeze.

He wanted to sleep now, but Sa-Ba had started talking again and he wanted to listen; so, he sat up straight and fought the urge to sleep.

"Eryion, I have loved you from the moment I learned of your birth. You mother and father were my very best friends. They were like my sister and brother. And we grew up here...here on Benaly Island."

With slurred words, Eryion replied, "Yo-ou meeeaaan...Beeennnnnaaaallllyyyyy Centre........."

"No, my son. I mean Benaly Island. Now: *Sun ọmọ mi, da mi ni wa ibi ... ibi ti a ti le jẹ ọkan[11].*"

Eryion instantly fell to the ground on the blankets and went into a deep sleep. Before slumber surrounded Sa-Ba, she whispered, "Eo wa lati awọn iwo ti awọn miran[12]." A mist fell upon them and she allowed herself to sleep.

Awaken, my child!

Sa-Ba sat with Eryion's head in her lap. He could hear Sa-Ba's voice, but something didn't feel right. He still felt the cool breeze around him but stronger than before. He opened his eyes to the most majestic thing he had ever seen in his entire life...Water! It was everywhere. It completely surrounded the Massive Tree.

---

[11] Sleep my son, join me in our place... where we can be one.
[12] Conceal us from the views of others

What's going on, Sa-Ba?

This is called a Dreamscape and we're on an alternate dimensional plane from Earth: Drome. Drome and Earth lay atop of each other in the concept of space: between Earth's stratosphere and the rest of the universe's space. Where we are on Earth, we are in the same place on Drome. I have brought you to Drome because I believe you are a True Dreamer and that you will have an experience tonight that will confirm your identity. If you have this dream, I want to be there and I want it to be better for you. The Dreamscape will allow me to share your dream with you.

Sa-Ba continued to explain. She looked around and then back to Eryion. He didn't look shocked like she expected. He looked calm...and possibly angry.

I waited until it was close to midnight...close to your birthday to perform this ritual. It was so different for me...when I had my first True Dreamscape... and I wasn't able to make the best decisions for my life. But before I tell you too much, we have to wait for...for someone to join us. It will happen soon. Save your questions, my inquisitive son.

Eryion had learned to follow Sa-Ba's scientific mumbo jumbo when he was a kid, so it wasn't like he was confused. He'd wanted answers. He'd come today to give her an ultimatum. He just didn't expect to get drugged.

He sat up. He thought about what she'd just said to him. Sa-Ba had called him her son. She'd never done that before. Her nephew...Her partner...Her apprentice even. But not her son. Instead of his usual response to her antics, he replied:

Sa-Ba, I always knew you were little weird, and I accepted that when I was a kid, but... this is just plain crazy. Am I dreaming right now? Is this real? Wait...Should I even be able to ask myself that in a dream? Give me a second to get myself together.

He stood up, looked around him, and then pinched his arm; he felt the sting of the pinch. He knew it wasn't a dream...but it was something else; it definitely wasn't reality. There was water directly in front of him and he could smell it: fresh and salty. He reached forward and touched it. Moist. Cool. Fresh. This was a fantasy that only existed in books.

Eryion, I've told you stories about Dreamers and Dromite Warriors before... since you were a boy. I've told you of Benaly "Island"...not the Centreland it has become.

I never believed that stuff, Sa-Ba! There haven't been islands like that in almost 100 years!!! Why would I believe that? Are you saying those stories were real?

Eryion felt the skepticism as well as belief occurring in his mind at the same time. Something felt right about everything Sa-Ba had always told him while he was here in this place, but something resisted it as well. He felt like there was more that he was missing. More to what she was saying that wasn't being said. Typical Sa-Ba: riddles and mysteries.

Yes, they were all real. The war was definitely real. Everything I've ever told you were my memories and they were all real. And this is happening now and definitely real. Because of my unique abilities, I am able to straddle both worlds. We are both on Earth and on Drome. I have left our bodies at the Massive Tree, while our minds and souls have traveled to Drome. We have manifested here...that's why I waited for everyone to leave the tree. If anyone were to move us from the Massive Tree, our hearts would stop and we would physically die leaving us permanently on Drome. Eryion, there are things that you and I can do in our dreams that other people can't. I wanted to "hijack", in a sense, your first dream state so that you wouldn't be afraid and I could guide your questions. The dream state would have happened with or without me, but with me...Well, when I was twelve years old, I had the same experience that you will have. I woke up and everything felt weird. But I had mine in the cottage...alone. It was so much more disorienting and I didn't have enough time...I didn't ask what I should have...I didn't know that I needed to ask anything at all. If you are a True Dreamer...as I suspect you to be... our ancestor, Aline Brown, will come to you and we can guide you together. You can have the help I didn't have.

Slowly, the world around them began to change. The water began to shimmer and various images began to appear before them. Before long, Eryion felt as if he were standing in the den of a cottage...a cottage that looked a lot like Sa-Ba's cottage. There wasn't a loft, but the layout looked exactly the same as the downstairs of Sa-Ba's cottage.

In the main den area, there was a make-shift bed with a young woman lying in it; the pallet of blankets under the Massive Tree had been in the exact same spot where the make-shift bed was now lying. Immediately, Eryion understood what Sa-Ba said about the experience being disorienting. Eryion looked at Sa-Ba and asked about the young woman,

Who's that?

Just wait...It's happening.

They watched as the young woman began to stir in the bed. She sat up and looked around while kneeling in the bed; she didn't seem to be as concerned as Eryion felt. She looked as if she was listening for someone. She stood up and walked towards them both. She began to reach forward as if feeling for something or someone. With extended hands, Sa-Ba intertwined one of her hands with one of the woman's hands while holding one of Eryion's hands with her free hand. Sa-Ba then told Eryion to hold the woman's other hand. They stood in a small circle of three and in a flash of bright light, the cottage began to shimmer and shake. Everything merged and became one place. The Massive Tree appeared in the middle of the den and water surrounded them.

> *Saran Moorlander, you have come to me tonight as a grown woman. It has been several years since we first encountered each other, and I have heard much of our family's future from our ancestors.*

Eryion listened through the woman's thick accent. He had never heard someone sound like the woman. She seemed to know Sa-Ba but called her by a strange name. A name that Eryion had heard before; but he couldn't remember when, where, or why he would have heard it.

> *But you, Saran, you continue to defy the prophecies and plans of the Creator. But I welcome you to this occasion, Saran Moorlander- "First" True Dreamer of Drome. So, your prophecy has come and gone, yet I am here and you are here... again...with?* Aline motioned towards Eryion.

Aline looked sideways at Eryion: taking measure of the man before her. She didn't say anything immediately, and

Eryion wasn't sure what was going on. He stood holding hands with the only mother he had known and a possible apparition.

The young woman continued:

This child has the gift of a True Dreamer, but...Aline looked closely at Eryion...he holds Warrior blood within him. He is clearly of my bloodline, but he possesses the blood of an ancient Gullivan as well? How is that possible? Saran, who have you brought to me?

This is Eryion Black. He is the son of...

Sa-Ba knew she was opening a door that could never be closed...

Eryck Brown and Yanieyl Starwell. He is my cousin, my nephew, and my son. He is the next True Dreamer. He is the one who can fix our world from the damage I caused.

As Eryion sat dumbfounded, listening to these two women, in this mystical place, he fought the urge to scream and run. But where would he go? Where was he? He wanted to speak. He wanted to ask questions. But there hadn't been anything that would prepare him for this world he was witnessing. 'Who's my Daddy?' just didn't seem to fit the occasion, so he didn't say anything. He followed his instinct...did what he had always done and just listened.

Aline, when I was twelve, you came to me. You gave me an idea that there were big things happening in my life. But you didn't tell me enough. You didn't tell me that it was bigger than even me. I wasn't prepared for my warrior. I wasn't prepared for my destiny. I made so many mistakes. Eryck made so many mistakes. Because we didn't know. When I went to Drome to train, I learned about the prophecy that ultimately led to the Great Water Recession. I wanted to change my fate and I wanted to change Eryck's fate, but I couldn't. So, when Yanieyl gave birth to this little boy, I took him from her when I saw the first signs that he was becoming a Principal Dreamer. I returned to Drome with him and began to study and prepare for a new world. When I came back, there was destruction everywhere. Dreamers and Warriors had destroyed Benaly... and Yanieyl... well it was too late for her or our world. All I could do was follow my instincts...which told me that Eryion would change things. He would be a True Dreamer. I knew that my destiny had changed...that my destiny was not to save Earth from the drought. It was to help rebuild it and raise the True Dreamers of Earth and lead them to greatness. To help restore humankind to a world of honesty and peace.

Eryion couldn't stand it anymore.

Honesty?!? Honesty is not looking like your strong suit. Sa-Ba, you know who my parents are and you've never even told me their names! Can you stop and tell me what the hell y'all are talking about?!? What's happening to me? Where are we? Who's the little lady? Sa-Ba, who is Saran Moorlander?

Aline spoke directly to Eryion then:

Young one, you are a True Dreamer, only the second to ever exist in the history of humankind. As Dreamers, we have been tasked with keeping the Earth alive, honest, and at peace. I am one of your ancestors from many centuries before your birth. In truth, I am one of the first of the Dreamers on Earth. Our life is one of sacrifice. We were created to motivate and inspire humans to be good and kind. We were created to help humans become the best of Ma-at's creations. It has not been as easy a task to motivate and encourage humans through their dreams. As a young child, I was told many things about my future children. I was given "special" visions to help the future generations of my bloodline. All of my visions of the past led to the birth and death of Saran Moorlander, your Sa-Ba.

She then turned to Saran:

I am sorry my daughter, but this is a time when I cannot help you. I am not prepared for this new future. You have changed too much. The thread of our lives lies in Eryion. The two of you are the last living humans from our clan...the last possibility to have Dreamers within our family.

Sa-Ba looked at Eryion and then to Aline.
But we aren't...Eryck...Eryion's father...he still lives. He is a warrior on Drome!

Eryion froze where he stood. The walls of the cottage began to shake. The water surrounding them began to rise turning into restless waves. Aline turned from Saran and spoke directly to Eryion:

You are stronger than any Dreamer I have ever experienced. If there is a chance for humankind, you...Eryion Black, son of Eryck and Yanieyl Brown...you are the key. Let Saran guide you. Find your father. Wait for your warrior. Grow to be the change our bloodline needs. I'm sorry we didn't have more time...

As soon as she finished, Eryion looked around to realize that he was standing at the base of the Massive Tree still holding Sa-Ba's hands. Eryion felt a burning sensation on his arm and looked down to see his skin pulsing and throbbing. It began to hurt tremendously and he grabbed around it with his free hand. He squeezed his wrist hoping to push out the pain. Sa-Ba placed her hand on his shoulder, "Accept the feeling, Eryion."

Soon the pain went away and he felt his wrist. A small brand had developed: dark and red. It was a heart shape. Through the middle of it, there appeared to be a lightning bolt piercing the middle of the heart as if shattering it.

"Eryion, your life is about to change forever. Now comes the hardest part...we wait."

Eryion stood flabbergasted. So much had happened to him in such a short time. This woman, who had raised him, knew who and where his father was. She knew his mother. She claimed to have loved them, and she had lied to him his entire life. She had discouraged him from ever looking for his family. He suppressed his anger and asked the most important question of the day. "Sa-Ba, you said my father was alive...Did you mean that?" He felt tears begin to sting his eyes.

"Yes, E," Sa-Ba spoke slowly and carefully. "He is alive; but until you have your Warrior, you...we can't see him."

Without any shame, Eryion exploded, "My warrior?!? What does that even mean?!? Sa-Ba, I can't believe that you have kept me from my mother and father all these years. I...I don't know how to feel. I'm so...."

"E, I want you to feel what is in your heart. Confusion... Frustration... Anger... Relief... Love. All of them are true emotions; but mostly, I want you to have felt loved. I promise you, E, you will learn everything you ever wanted to know. For everything I have kept, I can promise you that I will share that much more honesty from here on out. Just trust me." She looked for Eryion to show signs that they would be ok. She saw nothing but apprehension; she saw distrust.

She continued to try to soothe him. She spoke with the voice of one hundred years. She spoke like a guardian would.

"Ok...You wanna know what all this means? It means we're moving above ground. It means we move to the cottage and we prepare for a new world! A world where you are the savior...not the destroyer!"

Sa-Ba packed up their belongings and walked to the carriage without another word. Eryion held in his emotions. He looked at Sa-Ba walk way. He didn't know exactly what her words meant, but he followed behind her to the Vervoer. Neither of them spoke...but Eryion had many more questions...questions that needed to be answered. And answers he would receive! He *would* learn...he'd learn everything!

ALL ABOUT HER

Sweat...Urine...Dirt...Something else? What was that smell? The stench hit his nostrils as soon as he stepped on the porch of the Broken Oke. He'd never been there before...even when he turned 18 like all the other young boys underground. Sa-Ba said that the things that went on at the 'Oke were not dignified, and she wanted him to live his life in a dignified fashion. The fact that she wouldn't be caught dead in there only made Eryion want to be there even more. After two months of "training" for Sa-Ba...after two months of asking questions and getting no answers as usual...after two months of still not seeing his father...Eryion only wanted to do the exact opposite of what Sa-Ba would do.

On his best days, he was just upset with Sa-Ba for keeping so many secrets while he was young...for still keeping secrets even now. But on his worst days, days like today, he hated Sa-Ba...for everything she had taken from him and everything she still took. He was consumed with anger on the worst days. And today he was consumed to the brim.

He was a grown man! He could do whatever he wanted to do. He'd stayed home with Sa-Ba when he finished school unlike his peers who itched to see what lay beyond the confines of the Centrelands. Those boys had gotten into Onders and ridden off into the sunset. They hadn't worried about how the atmosphere would be different above ground. They hadn't worried about how they would find food. They were adventurous and brave.

Eryion wasn't. He'd stayed here because he believed in Sa-Ba. And now...well, now he wasn't so sure he believed in her anymore. So here he stood, at the most *least* likely place that he'd ever go.

"I'd like a drink of something," Eryion said as he walked up to the bar counter trying to sound like he knew what he was doing.

And older man with white hair and gray eyes looked at Eyion and laughed. "You wanna drink o' somethin'? Eh?" He turned around and continued to dry what looked like a dirty glass, completely ignoring Eryion's request. As Eryion studied the man, he noticed something very odd about him. First, he had an accent like his ancestor: Aline. He'd never heard anyone sound like that before his Dreamscape; but odder than his accent was his size.

The old man was fat, obese even. Eryion had never seen a person overweight before. There was very little food in the Centreland and what food there was, was healthy and divided into rations amongst families. But here, underground, stood a man who clearly weighed more than 300 pounds and was maybe six feet three inches.

"Well, are you gonna get me something?" Eryion asked, rather annoyed by the man's indifference.

The man threw his head back and bellowed, "Hell, naw! I ain't gettin' you nothin' to drink! There ain't a thang in heh for you, *boy*." He spat out the final word "boy" with disgust, and Eryion felt heat pulsate from his wrist.

"I got money *and* I've been old enough to drink for years. What's the problem?!?" Eryion couldn't understand why he would be refused service. For all practical accounts, he was a model citizen. He'd gotten in a little trouble as a youth for vandalizing but nothing major. All he wanted to do was branch out on his own, and now he was being refused service at a rundown bar?!

"You's Sa-Ba boy! I don't want nothin' to do witchu. She'll put a root on me faster than my head'll spin. And I ain't crossin' that woman!"

"How do you even know Sa-Ba? She wouldn't come in here if her life depended on it!"

"That's fo' sho, boy! That's-Fo-DAMN-Sho!" The old man laughed again. He found this to be hysterical. "I 'spected you round heh a few years back when ya come o' age. But sho nuff, ya never came 'round. Dem otha boys said you was respectable. Just like *she* wanted you to be. No grit 'bout you."

His laughter enraged Eryion. He felt the heat rising on his arm. He probably would have winced in pain had it not been for the atrocious words being used to describe him. He'd never thought of himself as weak. He just tried to honor the woman who raised him. It wasn't that he didn't want to do what the other kids did; he just knew those things were wrong. But he was grown now...right or wrong...he-could-do-whatever-he-wanted-to!

"Look, sir! I don't know nobody well enough for someone to say whether I got grit or not. What I know is that I got money and I wanna drink! Sa-Ba ain't even my momma! Can I get a drink or do I need to find another place?" Eryion was trying his hardest to sound like he had "grit," though in all honesty he wasn't really sure what "grit" really entailed.

"Ok, Ok...I ain't turnin' 'way no good money. 'Specially when ya full grown and all." The man looked around the bar, and then he smiled at Eryion revealing several gold and silver teeth, just another of the oddities about this man. "But if Sa-Ba finds out, you betta make it clear first thing! I 'on't need her bran' o' magic on my place. I seen what she can do!"

Eryion was confused by the man's description of Sa-Ba. He knew that people whispered about her and that there were rumors of witchcraft, but he'd never heard anyone speak of her with the conviction this man held. This man had witnessed Sa-Ba doing something that terrified him.

The man slid a clear mug to Eryion. He took a sip of the liquid and immediately felt as if his entire chest would burn and explode.

"Got a bite to it, don't it?" The old man laughed and several other men joined in. As Eryion choked on his drink, he wondered why people drank this stuff at all. But as he thought about it, he found himself laughing as well. His head began to feel lighter and heavier at the same time. He forgot about Sa-Ba. He forgot about training. He forgot about waiting on a Warrior. He felt his problems lift from his shoulders, if for only a moment.

"Yeah, I guess it does." Eryion smiled as he had his first drink in a nasty old bar.

The old man from Broken Oke was called Auction. For several weeks, Auction and Eryion had talked and discussed life in the Centrelands: Life underground as well as life above it. Auction had experienced so much more than Eryion. Before long, they had even become something like friends.

Auction told stories like Sa-Ba which made Eryion curious if Auction had a secret life too. But what he liked about Auction was that his secrets were open secrets. When Eryion would ask too many questions, Auction would just say, "That's nunya bizness!" And that would be it. Sa-Ba would give some mysterious reply that resulted in even more questions and no answers. Eryion respected Auction's evasion tactics a little more.

"Eryion, you been comin' 'round heh for a few weeks now, and ya think ya done learned a great deal 'bout liquor I 'spect. But in all my years, I ain't never known a man come 'round here that ain't got something he runnin' from. So, E, what *you* running from?"

Auction was an intelligent man. He'd never had formal education but you could tell he knew a lot. And he had an incredible intuition and memory. He remembered everything about Sa-Ba from when she first came underground. He was able to tell Eryion stories about his childhood. He even knew a few things that Eryion had forgotten. It made Eryion wonder what relationship Auction and Sa-Ba had held in the past. But either way, Auction knew everything about everyone. He'd say that everyone left their problems in the bottle. I guess he was ready for Eryion to start leaving his in there, too.

"I ain't tryin' to run you off, E. But I do gotta lot of respect for your auntie. And she's right almost 99.9% of the time about everything she pokes her nose into. So, if she didn't want you drinkin' and hangin' 'round the likes of me and these guys, I'm sho she gots a good reason. When you first come in, I didn't think it no harm to let you try a lil' hooch. But you almost like a regular now and I kinda feel some type a way 'bout it. Ya know?"

Eryion knew exactly what he meant. "You mean you're gonna tell Sa-Ba I've been coming here," Eryion said sounding defeated while Auction nodded. This was the one place that was his. He had created his own memories here. He had a friend here...at least he thought he did. But he also knew that people feared and respected his aunt. He didn't want his friend to fall out of grace with Sa-Ba.

"Auc, can you at least give me till tomorrow? I'll tell her myself, I promise. Just let me have this one night."

"You got it, E!"

When Auction turned around to fix his drink, Eryion began to feel a burning sensation on his wrist. He'd had moments where his brand on his wrist would tingle or burn. Usually it was at night when he was drifting off to sleep; those nights he would dream of his ancestors and learn more about himself and his family. But lately, it had been burning more when he came underground.

He looked around to see if there was anything unusual at the bar. He saw the typical guys gambling in the corner like usual. He saw the red headed lady who always came in for favors. He looked down the bar for Torke and Blade; there they sat with their drinks in hand. But right past Blade was a woman. Eryion had never seen her before.

She had long white hair with black highlights in the front. Though she was sitting, Eryion could tell that she was tall. She looked to be maybe six feet tall, maybe taller. She had almond shaped eyes that were jet black and she had the thickest eye lashes he had ever seen on a woman. Her lips were full and pink; they looked soft. The longer Eryion looked at the woman, the more his brand burned. He felt himself rising from his chair and walking towards her. He felt drawn to her. As he got close to her, he felt a cool breeze come over him.

"Eryion Black!"

Eryion snapped out of his daze and realized that he had been walking over to the woman. What was he thinking? What was he going to say? He'd never tried to talk to a girl before, let alone a woman! And who was that voice that brought him back to reality?

Eryion turned around to see a very infuriated Sa-Ba. He looked at Sa-Ba and gave her a half-smile, "Hey, Sa-Ba!" He tried to be calm and act as if everything was normal. It had taken the guys a while to accept him at the Broken Oke, and he really didn't want to prove them all right by his aunt dragging him out of the bar.

"Don't 'Hey, Sa-Ba' me! What are you doing here?!?"

"Awww, Sa-Ba, I'm hanging out with my friends. Having a drink. Would you like one?"

Eryion was still trying to maintain the façade of being cool...of having "grit."

"Your friends, huh? Who are your friends, E? Who?...Torke? No, wait, I bet Oscar is your BFF!" She pointed to one of the regular guys who gambled at Oke. "*Or*, are you gaining great wisdom from Auction, here?" She moved closer to the bar staring directly at Auction.

The entire time she spoke, it was if she knew that Auction was who Eryion came to see. There was chemistry between Auction and Sa-Ba that was almost tangible. She walked over with a smooth, sultry stride directly in front of Auction and spoke in a low voice that only the two of them could hear.

"How dare you serve my son in here?!? How dare you even speak to him?!?" Immediately, Eryion felt a rush of emotions. The first that registered was confusion from Sa-Ba proclaiming him as her son...again. No one in Benaly was ever confused about the nature of their relationship: she was aunt, he was nephew. The next was anger at Sa-Ba for ruining a place that he had finally begun to feel like a man in. But the last emotion was shock from the fear and anxiety on Auction's face. He actually looked petrified. Eryion had seen this man shut down the biggest and baddest men underground. But this little woman, standing all of 5'4", brought on a look of sheer terror in Auction.

"Sa-Ba, ya know I cain't turn down a good buck! Besides, he was gonna tell you hisself."

Sa-Ba wasn't satisfied, "How long?" This time she looked at Eryion. He'd never seen her like this. She wasn't scary to Eryion on a normal day; but from this point of view, he was literally shaking. Her voice was low and deadly. She brought about total silence in the Broken Oke; Eryion had never heard the Oke silent...even when it was closed.

"It's just been a few weeks, Sa-Ba. Barely a month." Eryion looked down before saying, "I'm a grown man, Sa-Ba."

Eryion wasn't sure how she would respond. Today was not a day he was enraged. Today was a day when he actually understood how complex his life was. That he understood the sacrifices Sa-Ba made for him. But at the same time, he enjoyed coming to the bar. He liked talking to Auction. He liked feeling like one of the guys. He liked having a life...a life of his own. He didn't want to fight her about this.

"Look Sa-Ba, I don't even give him the strong stuff!" Auction confessed to Sa-Ba, refusing to look at Eryion in the eyes.

"You what?!?" Eryion screamed. "Is it just second nature for *everyone* to lie? Why lie about that, Auction? Why?"

"Cuz you don't have no bizness drinkin' no real hooch, boy! I letcha try it the first time you was here. I thought it'd burn ya chest bad enuff that ya wouldn't come back. But you just kept on comin'. So, I been waterin' down the hooch and givin' ya light tea. It's gotta taste like hooch, but not as much of tha damage."

"Was anything you told me true?" Eryion looked at Auction with the hurt eyes of a young boy and the feelings of betrayal pressed into his mind.

"Eryion, I ain't never lied 'bout nothing but the hooch. I swear, and that wasn't no full lie. Hell, you can barely handle the light tea." Auction realized that he actually cared about Eryion. He didn't want Eryion to feel that he couldn't trust him. "But E, your auntie ain't been wrong 'bout nothing long as I known her. Ain't a man in here want you to switch places wit' em. Dat hooch is for those that's done lost it all. And, kid, you ain't had it all to lose just yet!"

"I'm not going with you, Sa-Ba. You might as well go on back up. I'll be home tonight like I am every night. But...but right now, I'm staying here."

Sa-Ba looked at Eryion at first with anger. He could tell she wanted to grab him by the arm and drag him out. But then her look became one of empathy...like she understood what he was going through and what he needed. Sa-Ba didn't say a word. She gave Auction another piercing glare; she turned around and walked out the Broken Oke. With her departure, Eryion lost the feeling of the cool breeze: the feeling of Sa-Ba.

But instead of there being no pain, the burning sensation returned and intensified. He looked around, but only the regular patrons remained. The double doors of the bar swung out as the mysterious woman walked out of the bar.

Eryion caught himself running to the door to catch her. He had to know who she was. When he reached the doors, there was no sign of her. The streets were full of people, but the white-haired woman was gone. Eryion felt an ache in his heart and wondered if she was the cause of it. He rubbed his brand and slowly walked down the underground street that led to his old home. The pain slowly subsiding.

When he reached his and Sa-Ba's old home underground, he felt relief. This place was familiar. He used his key to open the door. When he walked in, he was shocked to see that most of the furniture had been covered and there were boxes that lined the walls. Eryion didn't think that Sa-Ba had come back there since they had traveled to the Massive Tree months ago.

She didn't take her gifts to the Tree now that they lived above ground, but she visited the Tree every day. Sometimes, Eryion would follow her and catch her talking to the Tree like someone was there with her. Other times, she just sat silently alone.

He walked into his old house and went to his room. As he approached his bedroom door, he noticed a flicker of light and he thought he saw movement. With apprehension, he pushed the door open. To his surprise, the woman from the bar sat in a chair beside his bed. She sat with ease in his room as if she had lived there and not the other way around.

Eryion walked into the room. "Good evening. How may I help you?" He tried to sound nonchalant, but his body was trembling with anxiety. Who was this woman? How did she get into their house? He reached for his arm as his wrist began to burn uncontrollably. As he moved further into the room, he winced with pain that was beginning to rise up his arm and to his chest.

"The better question, Eryion, is whether I can help you." Her voice was melodic to Eryion's ears. But something about it held a hint of treachery. He felt apprehensive towards her, but something about her made him feel like he was at home. The burning continued as the woman stood up and walked towards Eryion. His first instinct was to back away from the woman. She gave a sly smile and a quiet smirk.

"Don't be afraid of me, Eryion Black. I will not hurt you." She continued to move close to him, and once she was as close as she could get, she quickly reached for his wrist where his brand was. He attempted to pull away but her grip was stronger than he could have imagined. She ran her fingers over the brand and said quietly, "Tunu inú si o[13]."

The burning began to subside and the woman looked into Eryion's eyes. When Eryion looked in her eyes, he felt as if he could see a galaxy of stars. He wasn't sure if he was dreaming, like his other dream states. He wasn't sure if he was having a Dreamscape and this woman had joined his dream like Sa-Ba had. He didn't know what was happening. As he continued to look into her eyes, Eryion felt himself being torn between wanting to follow this woman to the ends of the Earth and wanting to run like Hell was chasing him. He settled on simply pushing the woman away.

"Who are you? And what do you want?" Eryion asked coldly. The woman was taken aback by Eryion's rebuff and she stepped away quickly. He regretted his cold demeanor as soon as he'd responded, but it was too late.

---

[13] Calm feelings to you

"My name is Khoisan." She looked hurt as she hurriedly looked around the room. With a start, she focused on him again and continued, "I came to...You know what, I don't know why I came. Nevermind!" Khoisan pushed past Eryion towards the door.

"Wait!" Eryion protested.

As she rushed out the house, he heard her say, "This was such a mistake!"

One would have thought that the house was huge; but for such a small space, she moved like lightening. He couldn't get to her fast enough.

When Eryion arrived back at the cottage, Sa-Ba was awake, waiting for him in the den. She didn't look angry, but she didn't look happy either.

"So, did you drink your fill?" Sa-Ba asked sarcastically.

"No, Sa-Ba, I left not long after you. I went back to our house."

"Do you feel better now?"

Eryion walked over to the couch. He didn't want to fight. For over two months, he'd been experiencing new things every day. Talking to dead people in his dreams. Changing his diet to adjust to living above ground. Feeling like he and Sa-Ba were more like strangers than family. No, he didn't want to fight tonight. He wanted to have a normal conversation with his aunt that he loved. So, in a casual and nonchalant voice, Eryion spoke, "No, I don't feel better now. But, I met a girl. She was waiting for me at the house."

When Sa-Ba heard this, she sat up and the 'concerned parent' look covered her face.

"Who was it?" Sa-Ba actually sounded nervous. Eryion thought it was ironic that Sa-Ba was wearing the same nervous face that Auction wore just hours before. Who could make Sa-Ba nervous?

Eryion looked at Sa-Ba and said her name: "Khoisan."

Sa-Ba stood up and looked at Eryion with all the secrets that she kept hidden behind her eyes. She stood in front of Eryion and said four words: "Never See Her Again."

Sa-Ba went to her room and closed the door. Eryion went to the loft and sat on the edge of the bed. Who was Khoisan? And, why was Sa-Ba afraid of her? He'd heard Sa-Ba. He understood her warning, but he *would* see her again.

He had to see Khoisan.

KHOISAN

How could she be so stupid? What made her think that she should engage him? She was to observe only! Observe only! They would be angry with her for making her presence known sooner than they had planned. And what would he do? Would he tell her? Of course, he would tell her? He doesn't know anyone but *her*.

Khoisan stood in her apartment and wished that she had not been chosen for this assignment. It had been two days since she had seen Eryion. She'd always wanted a Dreamer of her own, but not a *True* Dreamer. There had only been one True Dreamer ever, and she had changed the world as everyone had known it; her Warrior had suffered for her mistakes. She had unveiled things that should have stayed hidden. She'd broken things that were not broken. Saran Moorlander: The True Dreamer of Legend.

And now, there were more of them coming. More True Dreamers that would be able to walk the planes of Drome:

defying time and life as it had always been known. Dromites were now beginning to become divided because of the idea of humans on Drome and what that would mean for Dromite and human relations. For the first time in the history of Drome, the world was filled with unrest...There was no sign peace.

In the beginning of time, Dreamers and Warriors were soul mates. Many fell in love and had children. It was believed that it was the only way to ensure Principal Dreamers continued to be born on Earth. The Browns of Earth were united with the Gullivans of Drome: two families that would work together to mold humans and society. These two families were thought to have possessed the perfect biological traits that would allow Drome and Earth to be connected.

Presumably, the Creator never thought that these families, the Browns and the Gullivans, would want to break free of each other...or that the other families on Drome would want to be Warriors to Dreamers on Earth...that other families on Earth would be worthy of becoming Dreamers. But all of the wants and desires of both humans and Dromites came into fruition, and war ensued on Earth between the Browns, Gullivans, and all other Dreamers and Warriors that had come to Earth under the reign of Queen Anya.

Many thought that all of humankind would die, but no one knew that humans could never be completely extinguished. There would always be humans that could survive any catastrophe. The only enemy of humankind would always be humankind itself. The war was the beginning of the consequences of the *last* True Dreamer.

After the war, the new king of Drome declared that Dromite Warriors assigned to Earth would have to be selected; the old way of sending Gullivan-born Dromites would end. Men and women had to go through additional years of training to become Earth Warriors, the new name of Dromites who trained Earth Dreamers only. He also forged a new agreement with the Creator, something that had never been done before in Earth or Dromite history.

No one had ever seen or contacted the Creator directly; the Creator had always been a mythological deity. But the new king actually met the Creator and they forged an agreement. In addition to the Earth Warriors' additional training, the agreement further held that Dreamers would be determined *after* their birth; it would no longer be a birthright through the Brown clan only. The Browns and Gullivans were no longer forever connected, and they were no longer the sole determinants of Earth's future.

The agreement also provided that the True Dreamer, Saran Moorlander, after 1000 Earth years, would vow to leave Earth forever. The consequence of her past failures would be to assist the Creator with overseeing the universe until the end of time: no longer connected to any humans or Dromites once in exile. Supposedly, there would never be another True Dreamer. That was supposed to be the agreement.

However, now, Khoisan had been assigned to a Dreamer...the next *True* Dreamer, or at least the only one suspected since Saran Moorlander. New rules had been established by the council for Dreamers and Warriors, but the new rules didn't prepare the council for another True Dreamer which meant that Khoisan didn't have the comfort of other Earth Warriors to aid her.

Time on Drome was not the same as Earth time. It moved both faster and slower at the same time. For Khoisan, she had lived almost 2000 Dromite years when she moved to Earth. And when she was finally chosen, she was excited. She had spent her entire life training to be an Earth Warrior. The problem was that her age on Earth only translated to 20 years of age. As a Dromite, she had been considered an adult at the age of 1200, but on Earth, she was treated like a child. This was the first major adjustment. She spent over two Earth years simply learning how to back track and live like a kid again.

Her next major transition was the lack of water. On Drome, the people have the power to create whatever they desire for the most part. The matter around them is easily manipulated. Drome would never run out of water. Drome was the World of Dreams for all living beings in the universe...not just Earth, but all other planets as well. She found that on Earth, she was constantly thirsty. Her skin felt scaly and dry every day. Living underground only made matters worse; she felt stifled as if she lived in a prison. She longed for the suns of Drome and fresh air. Things like this made it harder for the Earth Warriors.

So, to help Warriors with their transition, a new Dromite position had been created. There were some Dromites who specialized in Earth cultures; most were not Warriors and didn't have the affinity to be a Warrior. These Dromites and their families served as transitioning families for Earth Warriors to help them get acclimated. The head of a transitioning family was called the Orilede Olori[14]. The Olori acted as liaison between the Dream Councils on Drome and Earth. In addition, the Olori were expected to counsel and guide the Earth Warriors. Tatya was the Olori of Khoisan's transitioning family.

After several years of learning how to survive the physical and mental difficulties of living on Earth, Khoisan was finally given the name of her Dreamer: Eryion Black. Tatya had very little details about Eryion, only that he was to be observed only. Khoisan should never get too close and never let him see her. Khiosan had obeyed.

For months, she had followed this man around. Her first impression of Eryion was that he was weak and odd. His body was long and thin. He didn't have the body of a Warrior like

---

[14] Transitioning Leader

she was accustomed to. He was pale, but he also possessed a strange tan hue. He wore his hair long, unlike the other men underground. It was dark black and curly. His eyes were penetrating. He had large, light brown eyes with thick eyelashes. After time, she realized that she found him to be beautiful.

She wondered more and more about him. Why didn't he have any friends? Why didn't he do any of the social things that other men his age did? She knew that she had experienced much of life before him; but when she watched him, she felt as if she were waiting on her own life to begin.

Then, on his 21st birthday, it was revealed that he was a True Dreamer...that if taught, he could enter and survive on Drome as well as Earth. The revelation of his being a True Dreamer had both intrigued and terrified her.

Tatya had lurked around for weeks after Eryion's status had been discovered. She would follow Khoisan on her daily observations. Finally, Khoisan asked Tatya when she would be able to introduce herself to Eryion.

With agitation that Khoisan had never experienced from her Olori, Tatya responded, "We do not question the Council. We do as they ask. Just wait for further instructions and practice patience. It is a human virtue well worth your character."

Going to the Broken Oke was not part of the instructions she had been given. Speaking to Eryion...Telling Eryion her name...well, that was a direct defiance.

She didn't know what to do or what would happen.

***

Khoisan heard a tap at her door. She walked over to the door and peered through the peep hole expecting to see Tatya. Khoisan didn't have friends. She was surprised to see Eryion standing on the other side of the door. Her heart began to race. How did he know where she lived? Why had he come there? Maybe she could act like she wasn't home and he'd go away.

But, what if Tatya came while he was standing there? How could she explain his presence? He continued to knock and finally he spoke through the door.

"Khoisan, I can hear you breathing, and I heard you move. Open the door. Your neighbor already told me you were here."

Eryion's voice was deeper than she remembered from the night before. With surprising elation, she realized she could literally feel his presence. She could feel his heart beating on the other side of the door...almost as quickly as her own heart was beating in her chest. She reached for the door and slowly she felt as if an electric current were pulling her closer to it...closer to him.

When she opened the door, Eryion stood there and smiled a cocky smile. She stood there frozen until she realized that he wasn't smiling...he was grimacing.

"Eryion, what's wrong? Come in!"

"Who...are you? What's happening to me?" Eryion stumbled into Khoisan's apartment and landed on her couch. "I've had the burning sensations before. But ever since that night, I keep feeling like I'm dying...Like I'm being set on fire." He started to sit up, but he still held his brand tightly. "I didn't know what to do so I just started walking around and I ended up at the Massive Tree. The pain wouldn't stop. I came underground because you stopped the pain before. I thought maybe you could again." He paused and looked curiously at Khoisan.

"No one really knows you around here, by the way. That's kind of weird." He gripped his chest as he spoke to her.

Eryion continued to talk while Khoisan fixed him a drink to calm him. "As soon as I got underground the pain increased. I don't know how, but I knew it was because I was near you. I felt it at the Oke. I felt it at my house. So, I followed the burning; it led me here. The old man outside your apartment told me which door was yours."

"You just wandered the city until you felt like I would be near?" Khoisan asked, somewhat shocked. She knew that Warriors and Dreamers shared a strong bond. But normally, Warriors had to activate that bond. It didn't come instantly. That was how Khoisan had been able to watch him for so long without his knowledge. That night at the Oke was the first night he had ever noticed her.

"I didn't wander exactly...I came straight here. It was like I was being drawn to this building...drawn to you." Eryion began to stand up as he said this. He began to move closer to Khoisan. She noticed that as he moved closer to her, the easier it was for him. It was as if the pain was subsiding with every step he made in her direction.

"Eryion, you can't be here." She lifted her hands to push him away, and she began to move away. As she moved backwards, she noticed his face change. As she moved away, his pain began to increase. They *were* physically connected.

"Can you at least make the pain stop like you did before? Or tell me who you are...like who you are in connection to me? How did you get in my house the other night? I mean I'm not mad or anything...just curious." He looked at his brand and his hand on his chest, "and in pain as you can see. I know you can help me."

He continued to walk towards her. She could feel every word he said vibrating through her body. She felt compelled to tell him everything. She felt like she couldn't keep anything from him for any longer. She tried to speak, but her voice failed her.

"Khoisan." His voice was pleading. He needed her. Isn't that why she had gone through so much training? To teach her Dreamer. To support her Dreamer. All she had done was hide in the shadows. She was ready to step out of the shadows with this man. The mere sound of his voice melted her heart. He *was* her soul mate and she knew that in her heart.

With all of her strength, she forced herself to remember that she was the Warrior and he was the Dreamer. She was supposed to be the strong one. She finally found the words to say to him: "Orun, mi ife![15]." Khoisan caught him as he slumped over and she led him to the couch. Khoisan tried to think what she should do now.

Tatya would be furious; she couldn't call her. She couldn't call anyone from the council; the elders might even punish her for disobeying their rules. She didn't know what happened when you defied the council's orders. Finally, she called the only person she thought could help her.

"Hello?" She heard his scruffy voice on the other end, and she knew that he would have questions about her and how she got his number. He would have questions about her coming to him about this period. He repeated, "Hello? I don't do no practical jokin', Bub!"

"Don't hang up!" Khoisan finally said. "This is...um...well, I know you from the Oke. And I kinda need your help."

"Who da hell is this? Is this a joke? Did Torke put ya up to callin' me? I'm too old for this type o'..."

"No, it's not a joke, Mr. Auction...um...My name is Khoisan. I come in the Oke sometimes, and... I need your help...I need your help with Eyrion."

"Eyrion! Is he ok? Where are you?"

Khoisan gave her address to Auction, and she began pacing the floor. She thought of what she would say to him: something that would keep him from asking too many questions.

She heard three quick knocks at her door, and she rushed to the peep hole. Part of her still feared Tatya showing up through this whole ordeal. She opened the door to see the extremely large barkeep.

---

[15] Sleep my love

Auction was huge. Behind the bar, he looked big and tall. But in her apartment, he looked like a giant. His hands were large and didn't seem proportionate to his arms. His neck bulged like a Dromite Warrior in training. He did not look like a normal human; and for the first time, Khoisan wondered if he was.

"What'd you do to em?!?" Auction bellowed: his voice deep and powerful.

"I didn't do anything to him. He showed up at my apartment...I didn't know anyone that knew him but you. He passed out. Maybe he's drunk or something?" Khoisan tried to sound like a normal twenty-year-old girl from Benaly Centreland.

Auction eyed her with suspicion. "I knew this boy'd get me in trouble. Go on and tell me now, are you one of 'em too?" He asked her as if he knew about Drome and Dreamers. He looked at her like he knew as well.

"One of what?" Khoisan responded.

"Don't matter...you wouldn't tell me the truth no way. Y'all and ya secrets! Bunch a liars, ya are," he grumbled as he walked over to the couch. He lifted Eryion and slung him over his shoulder like he was a child. Eryion was thin, but he looked muscular and possibly heavy. But to Auction, he was like a little teddy bear. Auction looked back as he took Eryion through the door, "Look, at least tell me this...how long will it last?" He knew.

"Maybe an hour or two." Khoisan heard herself reply.

"An' will he 'member anything?" Auction sounded sad when he asked this.

"Probably not." Khoisan said as she closed the door behind Auction and Eryion.

Eryion wouldn't remember. He wouldn't remember coming there and he wouldn't remember meeting her two nights ago either. She had willed it through her sleep spell, and it would work.

When Sa-Ba's phone rang that night, she didn't expect to hear the voice of Allan "Auction" Okale. "Saran."

She hadn't heard anyone "alive" say her name in a century, aside from the times that Eryion asked her relentless questions and when her family came to her in her dreams, she was Sa-Ba: the witch of Benaly. But not to Auction.

She'd given him that name. The very first time he laid eyes on her, he told her that he'd auction his life away if he could spend one day with her. It was actually the first time she realized the mistake she had made when she committed to the new ruler of Drome and the Creator. But that was ages ago, why was he calling now?

"Allan. How can I help you?" She tried to sound formal; but, just as it had when she'd gone to the Broken Oke, her heart melted the moment she heard his voice.

"I need to bring Eyrion to you. But...I know you...well, I know you told me to never set foot on your land ever again. I can take him to your..." Sa-Ba interrupted Auction before he could finish.

"What do you mean you need to bring Eryion to me? Why can't he bring himself?" Sa-Ba could feel her anger and rage beginning to build up. She quickly fought her internal urges and circled her brand. She felt cool relief as she listened to Auction.

"I don't think ya want me talkin' over the phone. I can explain e'rything when I see ya, but you gotta tell me how I can get em to you," he paused and then said, "and if I am *allowed* ta bring em." He was deathly quiet after he said the last words.

Slowly Sa-Ba took a deep breathe. She had to remain calm. She had to remain in control.

"Auction, go to our house underground," she gave him the address to her underground apartment. "Use the spare key. You will know where to look when you get there. There is an Onder in the garage. You can bring him in that. I'll see you in an hour." Sa-Ba hung up before Auction could say anything else. She didn't want to sit and talk to him. It was going to be hard enough when he brought Eryion.

She knew that Eryion was ok. She could feel his life force. But she was nervous; she could feel the weight of anticipation of seeing Auction again. She could feel the weight of Eryion's destiny. Everything was coming together. Auction... Eryion... Khoisan... It was finally time to confront her past. It was time to right her wrongs. It was...time!

THE CIRCLE OF LIFE

It had been over an hour since Sa-Ba had talked to
Auction. She was nervous about Eryion. She was nervous
about seeing Auction again. Her pacing could have worn a hole
into the carpet. And, she had actually started to bite her nails- a
habit she had not had since she was 17 years old... almost a
century ago. She looked at the clock and time seemed to stand
still.

After two hours, she heard the Onder turn onto her long,
gravel driveway. It had gotten dark since he had called. She
stood at the door watching them drive past the small plants she
had begun to grow. They would become trees if everything
went according to plan. She felt her heart racing faster and
faster. She tried circling her brand, but it wasn't effective. She
knew that her heart, mind, and spirit were not connected at
that point. For the first time, she was actually afraid of what
was about to happen.

Both doors opened to the Onder. Sa-Ba looked
quizzically.

If he could get out on his own, why couldn't he drive himself? Eryion was scratching his head and looking like a teenager as he walked up the steps. When Eryion was younger, she had expected this type of scene: a tall, lanky boy coming home drunk from the bar. But, Eryion had never done things like the other boys. He had never done...*this*.

With her hands on her hips, Sa-Ba exclaimed, "Well, which of you idiots plan on telling me what happened?!?"

Eryion looked at Sa-Ba as if he were stuck in a fog. He came up the steps and looked at Sa-Ba with blank eyes.

"Heeeyyyyy, Sa-Ba!" He gave her a wet kiss on the cheek and walked right past her without another word. She looked at him flabbergasted and then turned her gaze on Auction. Her heart was *not* fluttering now.

"Awwww, Sa-Ba, now don't go doin' all that mumbo jumbo! I swear to ya...he ain't drunk and he ain't been back to tha Oke since y'all left the other night. Jus' give me a few minutes and I'll explain inside. I'm old and tired; I can't make that drive back tonight. Them cars are for the young ones."

Auction continued walking up the steps and he kissed Sa-Ba on the other cheek while grinning this time. She hadn't caught him off-guard as she had at the Oke. His kiss wasn't wet and sloppy either. His kiss was soft with hidden implications. She felt the warmth over her body, and she took a deep breath accepting that the worst of her fears was going to be realized tonight.

Sa-Ba fixed tea for all three of them. After Eryion continued to act strangely, Sa-Ba gave him another cup of tea with a special herb to help him sleep. Auction had sat quietly, watching Sa-Ba. He watched her interact with Eryion. Then he watched her clean around the house while they talked. He watched every move. She didn't have to catch him; she *felt* his eyes on her.

He hadn't actually drunk the tea, but he knew better than to be all out rude. While Eryion was awake, he had imitated sipping the tea. She picked up the cups that had been used for the tea. His was still relatively full; she wasn't offended. She made herself another cup.

"Three cups! Whoa now, Sa-Ba! Don't get too loose in here!" Auction slapped his leg and laughed. There was a hollowness in his laugh as if he only heard half of the joke.

"Allan Okale! Don't 'Sa-Ba' me. Eryion is sleep. You don't have to act like you don't know me. Tell me what happened to my boy."

Auction retold the events that had led to him picking up Eryion from Khoison's apartment. They had a history between them that prevented them from lying to each other. Well, it kept Auction from lying to Sa-Ba, but he knew that she would lie to protect her own if she had to. Sa-Ba paced the room, even more than she had while waiting for them to arrive.

"Saran...I mean Sa-Ba! Could you please stop pacing?" Auction tried to sound patient, but his lack of control over things involving Sa-Ba made him restless and easily annoyed. "Look, I know ya hate sharin' anything about your stupid lil' Dream world, but cain't ya at least tell me a lil a what is happenin'?"

Auction stood up and took Sa-Ba by the hands. She resisted initially, but he held tight. He knew how to hold her in a way that stopped her from fighting. It stopped her from wanting to be in control. He spoke softly at first, "Look, I know I told you I never wanted any part of this world, but somehow it keeps following me. Your spooks...they stay in my bar. Your boy, Eryion, came in...came straight for me."

He began to raise his voice slightly as his agitation increased. "And now this girl! I don't even know her. Ain't never seen her a day in my life... but she calls my phone talkin' 'bout she has Eryion! I know things didn't end right for us, and you haven't spoken to me in over fifteen years. But after one day of you back in my life, all hell done broke loose. I think I at least deserve to know what's going on."

Sa-Ba tried to turn away from him, but he tightened his grip. He was afraid of her powers, but he was also stubborn. He wanted to know what was going on.

"Woman! Look-At-Me!" As soon as he'd said it, he'd regretted it. He felt himself get weak in the arms and then legs as Sa-Ba's eyes began to glow. In a low voice that vibrated through his veins, Sa-Ba threatened, "Let me go or I will drain the life force out of you!"

This was the woman he had come to fear, not the woman he had fallen in love with as a boy. He cowered back, and her eyes stopped glowing. She began to cry.

"I'm sorry. I'm so sorry. Allan, I didn't mean to...I'm so sorry!" He could hear distress in her voice and remorse, but it didn't change the fear that returned. He slowly rose to his feet, a mix of emotions racing over him: fear, pain, doubt...but also love, sympathy, and faith. He didn't know how to handle her...he never really did.

He looked at her directly in her eyes. "Look, Saran, I just wanna know what I've gotten into. Is it more of this craziness or can I go back to my boring life? I mean, are strangers going to keep popping into my life?" He looked down and added quietly, "Will you?

"Allan, I don't know. Loving you...being *with* you. It cursed us both. I don't how much of this I can keep out of your life. I honestly don't know what will happen." Sa-Ba was being totally honest with Auction now; she had never been totally honest with anyone since she was a young girl. She wanted to tell him everything, but she had been taught that there was danger in revealing the Dream world to outsiders. In the past, her love for him was too great to allow him to be hurt by her world. But now, with the new ruler of Drome...with the presence of Khoisan...with all of the revelations that came with her agreement with the Creator...Sa-Ba just wasn't sure if she could keep him at a distance this time.

And if she couldn't keep him away, what would happen? How safe would he be? She decided to go with her heart; she opened up to Auction.

Reluctantly, Sa-Ba said, "Khoisan...I believe Khoisan may be Eryion's Warrior."

"You mean he's a Dreamer? The boy? But... but you said that he wasn't yours. That you had found him. When you came back...that's what you said." Auction sat down with a look of hurt and betrayal. Sa-Ba had never told him the truth when she left Benaly over twenty-five years ago, and she didn't tell him the truth when she returned many years later with a small child.

"Yes, Allan, he is a Dreamer... but I didn't lie to you. He is not my son." Auction breathed a heavy sigh of relief. Sa-Ba couldn't help but feel satisfaction at the realization that Auction still cared after all these years. "I believe Eryion is a very important Dreamer that will change the course of humankind...for the good. I brought him here to raise him, and I think he may be the key to the return of water on this planet..." Sa-Ba waited for a reaction from Auction.

He seemed totally unfazed by her comment. No one really believed that the world would ever have natural water on it again. No one could even imagine that much water period. The people of this world had never seen a sunset on the horizon of an ocean while sitting on the beach...they'd never seen a beach. They had never sailed the seas, surrounded by nothing but water...there were no seas. And, they never took lazy rides down riverbeds surrounded by trees or marsh...there were no rivers, few trees, and no marsh.

This world had never seen fields of beautiful green grass that grew after the spring rains or taken a drive through a mountain during the change from summer to fall to see the miracle of life in everything around them. There was very little rain or snow. There were very few breezes. The seasons didn't exist anymore. The humans of this time lived underground and in deserts. Everything on Earth was dry. That's all *these* humans knew. Auction couldn't even begin to comprehend what she was saying.

"Don't you understand what that would mean? People would be able to live above ground! Doesn't that matter to you?" Sa-Ba said with disbelief.

"What do you mean? You spent years talkin' to me in half-truths and lies. We from different worlds...different times. You've said some crazy things in the past. But I'm cursed? Water coming back? It just all sounds ridiculous! Tell me something that will make sense, Saran."

Her name. Her real name. It sent chills through her to hear him say her name. Sa-Ba looked guiltily to the ground. She'd become the girl who'd cried wolf...he didn't even believe her when she did tell the truth.

When she looked back up, her eyes were clouded with more secrets. Auction could feel it, but he didn't say anything. He allowed her the time she needed.

"No one will ever forgive me for what I've done to Earth. I don't know *how* to explain this to you. I've spent so much time concealing truths that I have forgotten how to be honest. I've forgotten how to share with another person." Sa-Ba looked to the loft. "I haven't even figured out how to tell Eryion everything."

Sa-Ba was trying to be honest. It was so hard when she had spent decades concealing the truth from everyone, including people she loved. She wanted to tell him everything. She wanted to share the truth. She had spent many years learning that truth was the most powerful thing in the universe. Whether on Drome or Earth, truth was the constant that connected living beings. Truth allowed for good, love, and peace to reign over evil, hatred, and war.

He deserved to know everything. Sa-Ba held the pain of concealment in her eyes. Auction could tell that it hurt her to keep secrets from him now just as it had years before. He knew this and wanted to comfort her. He wanted to wrap his large arms around her small body and tell her that everything would be ok. He wanted to...but he refused to touch her again. He knew without a doubt that he loved her...that he always had and always would. A small part of him knew that she loved him too, but the power that surged through her terrified him. And just as he was afraid to touch her, he also knew that he couldn't control his feelings when it came to her. Touching her would only send his emotions reeling. It would cloud his judgment and keep him from finding out the truth. He needed the truth now more than ever.

As he thought about this, she turned away from him. She walked towards the fireplace in the den and stopped near the window next to the fire.

"Allan," she started to tell him everything in that moment. She longed to touch him again. She longed for him to hold her...to take away the reality of everything. She wanted to ignore her training and follow her instincts...follow her heart. But as she had aged, she realized that her control over her powers and her emotions while she lived on Earth was becoming more and more unstable. Too much rage had almost hurt him before; too much love could do the same now. She couldn't trust herself to tell him the truth and then deal with the emotions that came with the honesty she would bestow.

She shook her head violently as she fought the internal conflict in her mind. Auction stood waiting after she had said his name. She turned around and walked back to the kitchen. She finished the cleaning she had started after Eryion had gone to sleep, and he realized he had lost her. Their honest moment was gone.

"Look, Auction, the couch pulls out. There are sheets on the mantle and towels in the bathroom for you. I'm going on to bed. I'll fix you breakfast in the morning and maybe we can talk more then."

She put the dish towel on the side of the sink and walked into her room. She closed the door slowly, leaving it cracked slightly. Auction noticed.

The next morning when Sa-Ba entered the den Auction was gone. The blankets and towels were neatly folded on the couch and there was a note:

Sa-Ba,

I left early. I want open honesty. I don't know if you can give me that. But, you know where to find me if you can.

Auc

She rushed to the door to see if he was really gone. The Onder was still there! She ran outside to see if Auction was still there, but there was no one outside. When she returned inside, she saw that the keys were still there. How would he get back?

Sa-Ba slowly sat on the couch and began to cry. She'd wanted to tell him everything this morning. She had meditated and thought through every word she would say. She knew exactly how to help him understand. She knew exactly what she wanted to do to *help* him understand. But he was gone. And she wasn't sure just how 'gone' he really was.

She never heard Eryion approach her from behind.

"Sa-Ba?" Eryion reached to touch Sa-Ba, but she reacted before he could. She turned on him quickly and grabbed him by the neck, "Mu ikú[16]!"

Eryion began to shudder as Sa-Ba realized what she had done. Her emotions had taken over. She tried to take it back, but she knew the power of her words. Eryion began shaking

---

[16] Bring death!

violently, seizing as he fell to the ground. He gripped his heart and gasped for air. She was killing him.

"Oh, my Creator! What have I done?!?" Sa-Ba lifted Eryion with amazing strength. She carried him to the Onder, not the Vervoer this time. She had to get to the Massive Tree immediately if she wanted to save him.

DEATH AT THE TREE

Sa-Ba rarely used the Onder, but she flew with lightning speed using the air controls to get to the Massive Tree faster. She had to get there in time. It was Eryion's only hope.

For fifteen years, Sa-Ba had controlled her powers while she was on Earth. When she had trained on Drome, she had become a master of Dromite powers. Even Dromites envied the Earthling who had greater powers than even the ruler of Drome. But on her trips back to Earth, she noticed that her emotions and senses were heightened. She struggled to maintain the same composure on Earth that she held on Drome. This caused her to lose control of her powers at times, making her dangerous and lethal.

Before she brought Eryion to Benaly when he was six years old, she had hurt many people on Earth with her powers, including Auction. She had spent decades of Earth time on other planets learning how to control her emotions while keeping her mind, body, and spirit connected. Until Eryion had been revealed as a True Dreamer, she'd had no problems. Sa-Ba had struggled with control over the past few months. Now, she had hurt the one person she loved the most on Earth.

"E, just hold tight! I'm going to get you somewhere safe." Eryion hadn't responded to her since she had shocked him. He had made a few sounds, but his breathing was extraordinarily shallow. If she hadn't been a Dreamer, she would not have been able to detect life in his body at all; but she felt his life force. She knew she still had a chance.

As she approached the Tree, she noticed the tourists that were gathered. She couldn't wait for them to leave. She had to get him to the Tree now. It was broad daylight. Everyone would see her carrying a grown man, though she was a mere five feet four inches. They would see her performing a ritual to bring him back. This would become a spectacle and be over all news and tabloids instantly which means the Councils would know instantly as well.

It would be hard for them not to interrupt, but Eryion's life was more important than worrying about who might see her. She would figure out the consequences after he was safe and alive.

As she made her decision she noticed in the middle of the crowd, standing close to the Tree, was a young girl with white hair frantically looking all around her. Sa-Ba knew instantly that it was Khoisan. As she hurried up the walk towards the Tree, people gasped and stared. Several men even asked where she was going and what she was doing. She ignored them. Khoisan finally turned around when she heard the commotion that Sa-Ba was creating. She ran to Sa-Ba quickly.

"What happened?!?" Khoisan asked hurriedly. She approached Sa-Ba and reached to touch Eryion's head. Sa-Ba pulled back defensively.

"Get away from him! This is all your fault!" Eryion stirred slightly and Sa-Ba knew it was because of Khoisan's presence. She felt bad for shifting the blame to Khoisan. She didn't want to admit it, but Khoisan was his Warrior and she could help Sa-Ba save Eryion. While still carrying Eryion, Sa-Ba jumped gingerly over the fence that now encircled the Tree: Khoisan followed her. The fence had been put up after Eryion's twenty-first birthday to keep people from doing exactly what Sa-Ba was doing now. She moved to the base of the Tree and laid Eryion down gently. She pulled out a vial with pink liquid. She lifted Eryion's head and poured the drink in his mouth. She then drank a vial of her own. She looked at Khoisan then.

"I need to save him." Sa-Ba looked vulnerable and apologetic. "You are his Warrior?" Sa-Ba struggled to ask this without sounding like she was spitting out venom. She hated the position the new ruler had placed her in. He had assigned Khoisan to Eryion on purpose. He knew what her presence would do to Sa-Ba. He wanted Sa-Ba to fail...he wanted Eryion to fail. That would not happen!

Khoisan knew Sa-Ba's reputation and history on Drome. She knew how Sa-Ba would feel about her. But she didn't say a word; she nodded a confirmation to Sa-Ba's question. Sa-Ba continued, "You will watch our bodies and keep us protected." It was not a question or a statement; it was an order.

Khoisan nodded again. Sa-Ba whispered quietly into Eryion's ear: "*Sun ọmọ mi, da mi ni wa ibi ... ibi ti a ti le je ọkan[17].*"

Sa-Ba slumped over Eryion's body. People were now starting to come closer to the Tree to see what was happening and before Khoisan knew it, there was a crowd. She had to protect them: her Dreamer and the first *True* Dreamer. She walked around the Tree chanting quietly: "*Bo yi aaye pẹlu ojiji ati òkunkun. Pa ọ ailewu kọja li oju awon ti o fẹ lati ri. Yọ gbogbo ìrántí ti akoko yi lati awon ti o yẹ ki o ko ri.[18]*"

---

[17] Sleep my son, join me in our place... where we can be one.
[18] Cover this space with shadow and darkness. Keep thee safe beyond the sight of those that wish to see. Remove all memories of this time from those who should not see.

Slowly, people that had been previously looking on with curiousity began to rub their eyes and shake their heads. She could see them through the cloaking encantation, but they could not see her or what was happening. She added the memory spell at the end so that the people would forget they had even seen Sa-Ba with Eryion. Until this moment, she hadn't realized that she wanted Sa-Ba to like her...to approve of her even. She would keep them protected.

Eryion awoke in the magical realm of Drome. Once he felt the fresh air and cool breeze, he instantly knew where he was. He looked around for Sa-Ba and there she stood against the Tree. She looked sad and... he couldn't quite place the other look on her face. Apprehension? Reserve? No...fear...he saw fear in her eyes.

Sa-Ba, why are we here? What happened? Are we at the Massive Tree?

Oh Eryion! I have done such a horrible thing. This morning, I...I attacked you.

Attacked?!? Eryion exclaimed.

It was an accident, Sa-Ba countered. *I didn't know you were behind me and I...I just reacted to your voice. I placed a death spell on you.*

A death spell?!? What does that mean?

It means that your human body is under attack because of a curse I created. Here in Drome, I can remove the curse; but on Earth, I didn't have that power.

Sa-Ba, I don't understand why you would do that. What happened?

This morning, I woke up to find Auction had already left the house. He and I had a...we had a disagreement. He left and didn't take the car so I wasn't sure what happened or who was in the house. When you walked up behind me, I just reacted. I was startled. I didn't mean to hurt you, I promise!

But a death spell? How do you even know how to do that? After everything with the dreams, not much surprises me, but you really being a witch does.

I'm not a witch. Having powers doesn't mean you are a witch. A witch is a negative term for people who "play" with mysticism. As Dreamers, we are all powerful. As a matter of fact, everything created by the Creator has power; but WE have a special connection to Earth that allows us to tap into our power more easily. I created the Death Curse during the War to save our people. But I'm NOT a witch.

As usual, Eryion felt like Sa-Ba had been keeping important secrets from him. He wore his frustration on his face as he peered into her eyes. He felt young and old at the same time. He felt naive and wise. He felt like he had always demonstrated patience with Sa-Ba...he had always given her room to be quirky and reclusive. But now, the secrets she kept were beginning to really affect his life. The life he was desperate to have. He wanted to meet his father. He wanted to meet this Warrior that was supposed to train him. He wanted to experience things that other men his age experienced. But he couldn't do that while he was unaware of so many important things.

Eryion, I know you are frustrated and there are so many things to tell you. I have kept the journals for decades for this very reason. My life has been long and hard, but one constant has always been my difficulty explaining our worlds and our way of life. For starters, on Drome, I have full control over my powers. I can do amazing things! Including removing this curse.

She walked towards him and placed her hand on his shoulder and calmly whispered: *Yọ gbogbo farapa, Ẹ daradara!*[19] Eryion felt a rush from his head through the rest of his body as she continued to explain.

I don't, however, have the same control on Earth. My emotions and feelings take over when I'm on Earth. Everything must be in sync to control powers on Earth: Mind, Body, and Spirit. Because I have not always been able to exercise control over my powers is just another reason why I never allowed myself to get too close to you...why I never tried to answer your questions. Love is an emotion I can't afford. Frustration is even worse.

Eryion reached for his chest and he remembered her placing the curse on him in that moment. He remembered being taken to the Massive Tree by Sa-Ba. Being carried like a small child when he was clearly two times her size. He remembered Auction bringing him home the night before and the strange interaction between Auction and Sa-Ba.

As he stood in this magical world, he couldn't help but feel like the only time Sa-Ba was honest with him was in his dreams or when they were here, on Drome. She was so much more relaxed and open. Now, he began to understand why. He started to say something to her...something to comfort her and let her know that he understood. He always understood her.

---

[19] Remove all hurt, Be well!

Eryion, we will not be here long. We had to share the potion and there was very little. I know now that I must be totally honest wth you. If no one else, I must be honest with you. And that will be hard for me. But we have to go now. When we return, Khoisan will be waiting for us and when we get home, I will let you read the journals.

Really?!? You'll let me read all of them.

Sa-Ba smiled. Eryion was excited about the idea of finally getting to read Sa-Ba's journals. But then, he realized that Sa-Ba had said someone would be waiting for them.

Wait...Khoisan? Who is that?

Sa-Ba was confused by his answer. She had assumed that Khoisan had revealed herself to him. Why else would she have been at the Tree? Surely she had come because she knew he was in distress. With that revelation, Sa-Ba regretted entrusting Khoisan with protection over their bodies. She did not hesitate. She immediately repeated the return spell: *Pada si ile.*[20]

When Sa-Ba opened her eyes, she saw the young woman with white hair running away from the tree. She looked down to see Eryion beginning to stir. It would take him longer to readjust.

"Khoisan!" Sa-Ba yelled, but the girl was too far. She had disappeared into the crowd. When Eryion opened his eyes, he asked one question: "Where is the person who watched us?" Sa-Ba looked from the direction Khoisan had run back to

---

[20] Return to home.

Eryion's inquisitive face. Now there was even more to explain, and she didn't even have the answers this time.

Once Khoisan saw Sa-Ba awaken, she ran away. She had forgotten that she had wiped Eryion's memory of her. She still didn't want Tatya to know that she had broken the rules. The best way to keep that secret was to allow her first meeting with Eryion to be genuine. She knew that Tatya would be watching when she gave Khoisan clearance to meet Eryion. She would know if Eryion had already met her. Warriors and Dreamers had that type of bond once the Warrior activated it. And their bond seemed to already be strong.

Sa-Ba would be angry. Khoisan wanted Sa-Ba to trust her, and this was not how she would gain her trust. But she had done what she'd said she would do. She had protected their bodies. She had shielded them from prying eyes. She had waited until she knew they were safe. Surely, Sa-Ba would understand. Khoisan hoped that Sa-Ba would not hold her personal feelings about Khoisan against her now that she was Eryion's Warrior. She had to hope for the best.

When she arrived at her apartment, her door was open. She readied herself for an intruder. She knew that no human could truly attack her, but she was prepared nonetheless. She stood silently outside the door listening for any movement. She heard none. She reached for the door to quietly push it open; but as she put her hand up, the door flung open and she was pulled inside.

She tried to fight the large man who had grabbed her, but he was too strong. When she finally stopped protesting, she was able to see that the man was a Dromite Warrior. She looked around to see five other Warriors standing in her living room. Of the other five, one stood out among the rest. He was tall with dark skin. He was extremely muscular...larger than the other Warriors in the room. As she walked towards him, she saw that he was standing in front of another man who was sitting in her lounge chair.

The man sitting wasn't large like the other Warriors; he was tall but thin. You could tell he was strong as his muscles protruded through his shirt. She imagined that he had zero body fat. The two men held evasive looks on their faces. She looked directly to the man sitting in the chair. She bowed to him formally, "King Yer, welcome to my home." She then turned to the largest Warrior who protected the ruler of Drome; she hid a warm smile and placed her fist over her heart. "General Black, it is an honor to see you again."

King Yer was the ruler that had changed Drome so drastically. He had usurped the previous queen when Khoisan was a baby on Drome. Many of the Dromites hated King Yer because he was said to be a human. No one could prove that he wasn't a Dromite and he had proven to be the strongest Warrior despite his size. He also had proven that he was the wisest and most strategic among those who believed they deserved the throne of Drome. No one challenged his ascent.

He stood up to greet Khoisan. She had heard many rumors about Yer that made her apprehensive... that he was cruel...that he was kind...that he hated all humans...that he loved all creatures big and small. His mysterious persona induced anxiety and suspicion in most Dromites, and now he was here in her apartment.

He spoke with power behind his voice though it was low and calm. "Khoisan of Drome. I have come to evaluate your progress with your Dreamer."

Khoisan was shocked at his declaration. "I'm sorry. I don't understand. I was told to only observe him."

Yer looked from Khoisan to General Black. Black merely shrugged his shoulders. Yer spoke again, "You have not revealed yourself to him?"

"Oh, well, I was directed by my Olori to wait, Your Highness."

Contemplating Khoisan's words, Yer rubbed his chin slowly. Khoisan looked from General Black to Yer. She immediately began to fear the repercussions of her actions. Should she tell King Yer the truth about everything that had happened between her and Eryion? Should she tell him about Sa-Ba and the Massive Tree? It wasn't necessarily a matter of whether she trusted the king; but more of a matter of disobeying the Councils and their orders, in addition to the consequences she would face for her defiance.

Most Dromites were unaware of the king's connection to the Councils on Drome and Earth. People speculated that Yer made all of the decisions, but it was also whispered that he favored a more democratic way of ruling. The fact that he was unaware of her orders made her uneasy and reluctant to tell him the entire truth.

Yer turned to General Black, "Who is her Olori? Was the Dreamer not awakened months ago?"

General Black looked unknowingly to Yer and replied, "Sir, I am unaware of the Council's orders in regards to her Dreamer. However, Tatya is her Olori. She is the best transitioner we have on Earth. She knows the Dreamer culture as well as the Earth culture better than all Dromites. I'm sure that if she told her to wait, there was good reason."

"Where is Tatya now?" Yer asked.

Khoisan wasn't sure and she realized that she hadn't seen or heard from Tatya in well over a week; that was abnormal. She now worried about her Olori: the strong woman who had been caring for her for so many Earth years.

"I have not heard from her in a little over a week, Your Magesty." Khoisan said quietly to keep from interrupting Yer and General Black's side conversation.

"A week!?!" General Black was taken aback by this. He turned to Khoisan and continued, "Where has she been? Have you been back to your transition home in those days?"

"No, sir. I have not. I have been observing my Dreamer as I was directed. And he has been...rather busy."

She decided to continue to withhold the truth for now. She would reveal as much as needed in the meantime.

General Black then turned back to Yer with worry on his face, "Sir, I believe something may have happened to Tatya. She was very concerned about Khoisan's Dreamer a few months ago and she had some strange speculations about him."

As Khoisan listened, she realized that King Yer could possibly be completely oblivious to Eryion's nature...that he was a True Dreamer. Or worse, Tatya may have learned even more information than Khoisan even knew. But it seemed that General Black had spoken to Tatya and didn't believe her; he seemed skeptic. Maybe that was why Tatya had not allowed Khoisan to approach Eryion? Maybe she wasn't supposed to be his Warrior afterall?

Months ago, it would have been a relief to receive a normal Dreamer; but now, she was connected to Eryion. She knew that she would irrevocably be connected to him.

Yer asked more questions about the speculations of Tatya, but General Black stated that he didn't think that Khoisan's apartment was the best place to speak about it. Black felt that it should be discussed in private, back on Drome. Yer reluctantly agreed. They stood to depart. Black whispered something in Yer's ear before all of the Warriors left her apartment. No one said another word to her as they all left...all but General Black.

Once the other Warriors had departed, General Black and Khoisan were left alone. He walked to her and pulled her into his arms. Though she was one of the strongest Warriors of her class, she was tiny and fragile in the arms of General Black. He kissed her lightly on her forehead and she began to cry.

"Oh, my iyebiye ọmọ[21], do not cry. It will be ok."

"Father, I am not doing well here. I am not a good Warrior. What will they do to me if I fail? And what about Tatya?"

"Khoisan, Khoisan, please calm down. You are a great Warrior. You must give yourself time. Being a Warrior to Eryion will come naturally to you. I promise. You were selected because you can do this. I will always watch for you and keep you protected, so have no fear." Khoisan dried her tears as she looked into her father's eyes.

"Does King Yer know who I am?"

"Yes, he is aware that you are my daughter. However, the Councils nor the other Dromites are aware. It is imperative that you keep that fact a secret. People will try to harm you if they know you are my daughter...especially Saran Moorlander. Do NOT underestimate her! She is strong...powerful...and most of all, Khoisan, she is dangerous! She isn't to be trusted!"

"I understand, Father." As she said this, Yer re-entered the apartment.

"Pherron, we must depart before the humans notice us. Let us go!" King Yer left once again followed by her father: Pherron Black, the General of the Dromite Army.

---

[21] Precious child

PERSONAL ACKNOWLEDGMENTS

Several people were driving influences in the completion of this book:

Toriano D. Green: My love, my friend, my partner... My WARRIOR! You believe in me. You believe in my Dreams. You are truly my BETTER half. I would be no where without you.

Julie Cassandra Brown Williams: My mother, who inspired me to begin writing again. You are the Superwoman I hope to become!

Jacqueline Brown Dukes: My aunt, who interpreted my dreams throughout high school and college...You were my ride or die no matter who I was at various points in my life. I know I can find you in my Dreams.

Abigail Brown "Grandma Abby": Though I never met you, you gave me the vision for Drome. You inspired your children who passed down your beliefs to many generations after you.

Rheadawn Brown: My first fan...My #1 fan. You forced me to write this book, whether I wanted to or not. You were ready every morning for a new chapter and encouraged me to keep going on to the next volume. Volume II coming soon thanks to Brown!

Demiana Barsoum: My FIRST student fan. You were the very first student to take a chance on your crazy teacher. I can't thank you enough for giving me that extra push. You are a Warrior to me!

Last but not least, I thank the **Creator** for giving me life. For continuing my life when I wanted to give up. For making me the person I am today, tomorrow, and forever! Honor and Glory to the One on High!

Drome Chronicles, Volume II Preview
Story One: Saran Moorlander
A True Dreamer's Awakening

ROYAL ENCOUNTERS

She lay there, still and calm. She was afraid to open her eyes. She hadn't expected to hear the dirt being packed down on the bed-like coffin. She thought when she "fell asleep" that she wouldn't know what was happening to her...but she was wrong. She heard her grandmother and Everett Gullivan chanting in the foreign language of the Dromites. She heard them lower her and her Warrior into the ground. She heard them bury her. She heard it all and there was nothing she could do about it.

For the first time, she questioned what was happening to her...her role as a True Dreamer. When she'd looked into the eyes of Pherron Black...the eyes of her Nana...she felt like she was making the right decision...that everything would be ok. But would it be? What if she had walked blindly into this? What if she really died? What if Eryck had been right about everything?

She tried to move her arms, but found she was immobile. She tried to speak to Pherron, but she couldn't speak out loud or in her head. Saran Moorlander was utterly alone. Her chest began to tighten and she realized that her breathing was beginning to get shallow. She knew instantly that she was dying.

She was buried alive.

Pherron could sense Saran's uneasiness. She was freaking out. He knew it would be hard, but they'd had very little time to explain everything to her before the ceremony. Under normal circumstances, he would have had months to mentally prepare a Dreamer for their destiny. Under normal circumstances, a Dreamer would train on Earth where things were familiar; but Saran wasn't normal. And this training would be unprecedented.

The purpose of a Warrior was to bridge the gap between worlds. Humans could not live on Drome. It required a mental stability that humans did not possess. Drome was a unique world. It was tethered to Earth's atmosphere, but it was also a conduit to all living creations on every planet in the universe. Drome could not exist without the presence of Earth; Earth could not survive without the powers of Dromites. It was a Catch 22; they worked together. That connection fueled all living things on every planet in the cosmos.

The depletion of water on Earth was directly connected to the fact that Dreamers and Dromites were no longer agreeing on their purpose...they weren't connecting. The imagination of humans was deteriorating and they were becoming completely reliant on technology, and technology was killing the planet. The natural resources that were used to maintain the lifestyle of the 21st century man were exhausting. And there were no real signs that the planet could survive it.

No one on Drome knew what would happen to their own planet if humankind ended...if Earth died. And most Dromites were oblivious to the looming threat of impending annihilation. Would Drome still exist in the universe if there was no planet to stay tethered to? Would the universe even exist?

Saran was supposed to be the key to this. Pherron had been told over and over again. He'd spent years learning to love Saran Moorlander, even before he knew her...before he'd ever seen her. His mother had told him that she was his destiny. Most of his life was spent knowing that he would be the Warrior to the first True Dreamer: The first human to walk the planes of Drome. And now, the time had come and the burden was heavier than expected.

He knew that Saran had to learn to control the powers she possessed. She had to learn to bring the humans and Dromites together again. Without being on one accord, Earth could not continue as it had for billions of years...it might not last another century at the current rate of things.

He had believed that Saran was strong when he first met her. She had survived their initial Dreamscape. She had demonstrated the strength to break away from everyone she loved or cared about. She had shown courage by standing proudly with him. But, was she strong enough for Drome? Was she strong enough for the training that could break even the strongest of Dromites? Only time would tell, and Pherron wasn't sure if they had that much time to wait.

After activating their bond, Saran's life force longed to be on Drome just as it longed to be on Earth. The moment he had seen her and their eyes had locked, her life force began to reach for Drome. Pherron had never seen anything like it. Her body literally fought her life force as she straddled the two worlds when they first met...something her body just could not handle. Now, they mentally and spiritually passing through to Drome to train her...prematurely...to make her the savior she was destined to be. Now, they were in a Dromite coffin and he wasn't sure that she really was strong enough.

He felt Saran's heart racing. He felt her anxiety and doubts. These were feelings of a human. Dromite training was not meant for humans. Her emotions could very easily be the end of her. He worried.

He worried that he wouldn't be able to fulfill his task as a Warrior. That he wouldn't be able to show her everything she needed to learn. He worried that he didn't know enough about humans to properly train her. He couldn't tell Saran that he wasn't even confident in himself...that he had failed before and it had ended horribly.

He worried.

He tried to squeeze her hand...reach into her mind for comfort, but he couldn't. He was completely shut off from her. That realization hurt him at his core. He had reassured her that he would never leave her side...that he would always be available to her. He needed to be there for her now, and he couldn't. For the second time in his life, Pherron Black felt like an absolute failure and he worried.

After what seemed like an eternity, Saran realized that she could feel something. Something familiar. A breeze? She then realized that she could smell the ocean. Underground? There was no way that she was still underground. The excitement began to overwhelm her. She attempted to wiggle her fingers and found that she could. She was afraid to open her eyes and find darkness, so she attempted to reach for Pherron only to realize that their hands were still interlocked as they had been when the bedlike-coffin was closed. She turned her head and began to slowly open her eyes.

She opened one eye and then the other. To her surprise, Pherron lay beside her smiling his cocky smile, holding her hand reassuringly.

"She lives," he said in a calm and comforting deep voice, but his eyes showed his concern.

"It looks that way," Saran said as she sat up.